"Lydia." He touched the back of his fingers lightly against her cheek. "I think we need to talk."

Uh-oh. Here it came.

"I need to be fair with you, Lydia. Whatever this thing is between us—and I can't explain it, either—I can't offer you a future. But there's no reason why we can't have a mad fling and blow each other's minds for the next few days. Well, apart from the fact that I'm your boss, and ethically that makes this completely wrong."

But at that precise moment he couldn't give a damn about ethics.

The only thing that filled his head was the need to touch her again.

"I have a suggestion." He paused. "We spend a week here. Together. And this thing between us...we can get it out of our systems."

"You're saying we should have an affair?"

"With limits. So we know the deal right from the start."

"An affair," she repeated. "For a week. A seven-night stand."

"Put like that, it sounds tacky." He grimaced. "I'm trying not to be dishonorable. I can't offer you more than an affair, Lydia. I can't offer *anyone* more than that."

She licked her lower lip, and he almost lost control again.

"This is mad," she whispered. "You're my *boss*."

Dear Reader,

Dramatic, passionate stories; charismatic, masterful heroes; wealth and glamour; stunning international locations—everything we love about Presents! Now two books a month are all that you expect from Presents, but with a sassy, sexy, flirty attitude!

All year you'll find these exciting new books from an array of vibrant, sparkling authors such as Kate Hardy, Heidi Rice, Kimberly Lang, Natalie Anderson and Robyn Grady. This month, Kate Hardy's *Temporary Boss, Permanent Mistress* fizzes with sparky sensual tension between a billionaire shipping tycoon and his feisty senior lawyer, Lydia. And in *Bought: Damsel in Distress,* a debut by Lucy King, heroine Emily Marchmont finds her sister has put her up for auction on the internet! Soon she's on a private jet heading for a sizzling date with the highest bidder! Luckily he's the sexiest man she's ever met....

Next month there's more sizzle and sass from talented Atlanta author Kimberly Lang with *Magnate's Mistress...Accidentally Pregnant!* And for sun, sea and sex, don't miss *Marriage: For Business or Pleasure?* by Australian author Nicola Marsh.

We'd love to hear what you think of these novels; why not drop us a line at Presents@hmb.co.uk.

With best wishes,

The Editors

Kate Hardy

TEMPORARY BOSS, PERMANENT MISTRESS

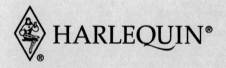

HARLEQUIN®

TORONTO • NEW YORK • LONDON
AMSTERDAM • PARIS • SYDNEY • HAMBURG
STOCKHOLM • ATHENS • TOKYO • MILAN • MADRID
PRAGUE • WARSAW • BUDAPEST • AUCKLAND

Recycling programs
for this product may
not exist in your area.

ISBN-13: 978-0-373-23653-4

TEMPORARY BOSS, PERMANENT MISTRESS

First North American Publication 2010.

Copyright © 2009 by Kate Hardy.

All about the author...
Kate Hardy

KATE HARDY lives in Norwich, in the east of England with her husband, two young children and too many books to count! When she's not busy writing romance or researching local history, she helps out at her children's schools; she's a school governor and chair of the PTA. She also loves cooking—see if you can spot the recipes sneaked into her books! (They're also on her Web site, along with extracts and the stories behind the books.)

Writing for romance fiction has been a dream come true for Kate—something she wanted to do ever since she was twelve. She's been writing Harlequin Medical™ Romances for nearly five years now. She says it's the best of all worlds because she gets to learn lots of new things when she's researching the background to a book. Add a touch of passion, drama and danger, a new gorgeous hero every time, and it's the perfect job!

Kate is always delighted to hear from readers, so do visit her at www.katehardy.com.

CHAPTER ONE

'MATT rang in first thing this morning. The kids have brought a bug home from school and he's been throwing up practically all night—he doesn't think he'll be back until Friday at the earliest,' Judith explained apologetically.

It was much better that the head of the legal department should stay at home rather than struggle into work and share the virus with his colleagues. Jake had no problem with that. He didn't bother asking about Adam, because he already knew where Matt's second in command was. On paternity leave.

Babies and kids everywhere.

Everywhere except…

He pushed the thought away. With Matt away, he needed to make alternative arrangements. 'So that leaves Lydia and Tim.'

'I'm sorry.' The secretary made a face, looking embarrassed. 'They're both at lunch right now.'

'Don't keep apologising. It's not your fault.' Jake frowned. He could reschedule the trip to Norway, but he was keen to get this deal sorted. And out of the two remaining members of the legal team…Tim could talk the talk, all right, but he didn't have Lydia's experience or knowledge, and he was perhaps a little too hungry for results. Jake needed someone calm, someone confident, someone who would pay attention to detail.

'Lydia will have to do. Ask her to come and see me when she gets back from lunch, would you, please?'

'Yes, Mr Ande—'

'Jake,' he cut in gently. 'We don't do formality at Andersen's.' It was the first thing he'd changed, the day his father retired and he took over as CEO: dropping the formality and opening things up a bit. But, nearly two years later, some of the staff still hadn't quite got used to calling the boss by his first name.

'Yes, M—Jake,' the secretary corrected herself quickly.

'Thank you, Judith.' He gave her a swift smile, and headed for his office.

Lydia will have to do.

That said it all.

And it rankled, even though Lydia acknowledged the justice of the remark. Jakob Andersen was sharp enough to know exactly what was going on in every single division of the company. To know what every member of his staff was capable of doing, to know what worked and what didn't, and where things needed moving around. He'd spent six months working in each department before he'd taken over as CEO, so he knew what every part of the company did and what challenges his employees faced. Anyone who'd been tempted to grumble that he'd only walked into the job because he was the boss's son had quickly changed their minds. Jake wasn't a delegator who spent all his time wafting around or in long lunches. He was a hands-on leader who saw what needed doing and made sure it was done and, if need be, he rolled up his sleeves and did it himself.

So doubtless he'd already spotted that Lydia Sheridan just wasn't cut out to be a corporate lawyer.

Lydia had the right background and the right training. What she didn't have was the shark instinct.

She'd been trying to kid herself for years. Trying to be the child her parents had wanted. Trying to be the person everyone else wanted her to be. Now, maybe, she thought, it was time to stop trying and just be herself.

So she would go to see Jake, at his request. But she had a feeling that he wasn't going to like what she was going to say. Because Lydia Sheridan wasn't going to 'do' at all.

'Oh, good, Lydia, you're back,' Judith said as she walked into the reception area. 'The CEO just came by—he wants to see you asap.'

'Sure.' Lydia summoned a smile. It wasn't Judith's fault that Lydia wasn't cut out for her job, so she wasn't going to take out her frustrations on the departmental secretary. 'I'll go now.'

When she reached Jake's office, his door was wide open, but she knocked anyway.

He looked up from his desk. 'Come in. Take a seat.'

As always, she found herself assessing him, itching to pick up pastels and a sketchpad and start drawing him. Jakob Andersen was simply beautiful. His piercing blue eyes demanded—no, *commanded*—attention and, teamed with his dark spiky hair and pale Nordic skin, were absolutely stunning. Though his face was maybe a little too thin and angular, and the slight dark smudges beneath his eyes said that he drove himself too hard. Since his two-month sabbatical, eighteen months before, he'd put in ridiculous hours. From what Lydia had heard, he was always the first one in the office and the last to leave.

What was he running from?

Not that it was any of her business. Besides, she wasn't supposed to be wool-gathering. He'd summoned her, which no doubt meant he needed her to sort out some legal nicety for him.

She sat down on the chair he'd indicated. 'Judith said you wanted to see me.'

'I have to go to Norway tomorrow to sort out some contracts. I need you to come with me.'

Abrupt and straight to the point.

Only…she wasn't quite buying this. Not after what she'd heard him say to Judith. And, given the reason she'd already decided to see him, she didn't need to be polite and pussyfoot around. She could be just as straight—all the way back. 'You need me.'

He frowned, clearly picking up the scorn in her tone. 'Yes.'

'That's a bit hard to believe,' she said.

His frown deepened. 'Meaning?'

'I overheard you saying that I'd have to do.'

He leaned back in his chair and raked a hand through his hair. 'Ah. That.'

At least he wasn't denying it.

'Actually, I didn't mean it quite in that way,' he said.

'No?'

'No. I admit, you're not my first choice,' he said. 'I'd arranged to go with Matt, but he's off sick and Adam's away. I know that both of them have dealt with this kind of thing before, and Matt speaks Norwegian, so it would have saved some time. But it's no matter. I'll translate for you, where necessary.'

'There's no need.'

It was his turn to question her. 'You speak Norwegian?'

'No. I was going to come and see you anyway, this afternoon,' she said quietly. 'To hand in my notice.'

He blinked, obviously taken by surprise. 'Why?'

'Because you're right. I'm not cut out to be a corporate lawyer.'

'I didn't say *that*. At all.' He looked straight at her. 'Your work is meticulous, Lydia.'

Because she made damn sure it was. It was a point of pride. Her work wasn't the problem. *She* was. 'I'm not like Tim—I'm not hungry to win.'

'Tim,' he said, 'would be completely the wrong lawyer for this deal. He needs to tone down.'

What? Weren't all corporate lawyers supposed to be driven, hungry for success? 'How do you mean, tone down?' she asked carefully.

'He needs to be able to sum up a situation quickly and know the right tactics to use—when to take it softly and when to push. If you go in with high-pressure tactics in Norway, you'll lose out. I need someone who's calm and competent, who knows the facts and will cut through the hype, and who'll meet deadlines and commitments.' He ticked the requirements off on his fingers. 'Someone straightforward. From what Matt tells me of your work, you're perfectly capable of all that, or you wouldn't be working at Andersen's.' His gaze met hers. 'Your problem is, you lack confidence.'

How would he know? Although she was aware that he'd spent time working in the legal department, it had been before she'd joined the company. She'd only ever worked with him on projects as part of a larger team, never one-to-one.

Before she had the chance to protest, he added, 'You're good enough to do the job; you just don't think you are. You need to work on that. I'll tell

Adam to add that to your objectives at your next appraisal and send you on some assertiveness training.'

Businesslike and to the point. And Lydia felt as if she'd been steamrollered. This wasn't how the conversation was supposed to go. At all. He thought she'd got cold feet, was having a minor confidence wobble? That wasn't the half of it. 'I was trying to resign,' she reminded him.

'I know. And I'm not accepting your resignation. Apart from the fact that the legal team is under strength right now—so it'd put us in a mess if I let you go—you do your job well. So there's no reason for you to leave.' He rested both elbows on his desk, steepling his fingers, and looked her straight in the eye. 'Unless you've had a better offer elsewhere?'

This was her cue to negotiate a pay rise. To claim that she'd been offered a huge salary and longer holidays with a rival company, so Jake would offer to match the deal.

Except… She wasn't a shark.

This wasn't about negotiating more money.

This was about facing what she'd known even before she took the job. About finding her real place in the world. The timing was all wrong, she knew—who in their right mind would leave a steady job to chase a dream, in the middle of a recession?

But it wasn't as if she had any dependants.

And she had savings.

She'd manage.

'No, I haven't had a better offer,' she said quietly. At least, not 'better' in the way that any business-man would see it.

Concern flickered in his face. 'Is there a problem you're not telling me about? Harassment of any sort?'

'Of course not.' She found Tim a bit wearing, for precisely the reasons that Jake had outlined, but she enjoyed working with Matt and Adam.

'Then I don't see any reason for you to resign. Except maybe the fact that you're undervaluing yourself.'

Maybe she was. Which was why she'd become a lawyer in the first place. In some ways, although it had meant years of hard work, it had been an easier option. Easier to give in instead of being stubborn and holding out for what she knew she really wanted out of life. To paint. She'd wanted to paint for years, but when she'd told her parents she wanted to take Art as one of her A levels they'd reacted badly. Why would the daughter of a QC and a top solicitor want to become an artist—to go and starve in a Parisian garret, doing a job that wouldn't even pay her rent? Ridiculous. And they'd refused to listen to her art teacher, too.

So she'd tried to please them. She'd studied History and Economics and Law, ending up with top marks and a place to read law at university. She'd trained as a solicitor and found herself a job as a cor-porate lawyer.

And she'd kept her sketching a secret between herself and her godmother, Polly.

'I don't want to be a lawyer any more,' she said.

He leaned back in his chair. 'You've fallen out of love with your job? It happens.'

He actually seemed to understand—and she really hadn't expected that. So Jake knew other people who'd reached a point in their career where they just stopped wanting to do it?

Almost as if she'd asked the question out loud, he said, 'Been there, done that, myself.' For a brief moment, there was something in his eyes, but he'd masked it before she could read it. 'And the way round it is to give yourself a new challenge. I think this job might do that for you.'

She wasn't convinced. She'd stopped loving what she did a long time ago. If she was honest, she'd never really loved it in the first place. She'd just done it because she'd thought it was the right thing to do.

And over the years it had begun to feel so very much the wrong thing. She didn't see how she could ever fall in love with her job again. 'What if it doesn't?'

'Do this one job for me,' he said, 'and if you still feel the same way afterwards, then I'll accept your resignation—backdated to today.'

Put that way, it seemed reasonable. And what difference would another few days make? 'All right.'

He glanced at his watch. 'I imagine this gives

you enough time to rearrange your meetings for the next couple of days?'

'Yes.'

'Good. Now, clothes.' He appraised her. 'Your suit's fine for business. We'll be in the south of the country, so it won't be quite as cold as the north, but you'll still need a windproof coat and boots—do you have any?'

Jake clearly didn't believe in social chat. And this was the longest conversation Lydia could remember having with him. It was the only meeting she'd had with him, one-to-one, in the three years she'd been working at Andersen's; though she remembered he'd been just as incisive in the presentations and meetings she'd attended along with Matt or Adam.

'Coat and boots?' he repeated, raising his eyebrows.

Oh, great. Now he'd think she had the attention span of a gnat. 'Yes, I have a coat and boots.'

'Good.'

'How long are we going for?'

'Until Friday—though if there are complications we might need to work on Saturday morning and fly back on Sunday. Have you been to Norway before?'

'No. Though I've always wanted to see the fjords and the Northern Lights,' she admitted. To sketch them—to capture the pure, clean Nordic light in pastels.

He regarded her thoughtfully. 'If you wanted to stay for a couple of days afterwards and take the chance to do a bit of sightseeing, I can arrange for you to have an open return flight. Andersen's will pick up your hotel bill, to make up for eating into your weekend and evenings.'

That was an offer she definitely wasn't going to refuse. 'Thank you. I appreciate that. Though I'd better call Matt and check it's OK for me to take time off next week.'

'Sure. I'll get Ingrid to sort out the travel details and let you know what's happening.'

It was a dismissal. Polite enough, but still a dismissal. She smiled politely, and left his office.

Jake couldn't settle back to work when Lydia had gone; every time he looked at the figures on his computer screen, his mind kept supplying a picture of Lydia.

On the face of it, Lydia Sheridan was the perfect corporate lawyer, with her power business suit, her mid-brown hair groomed into a sleek, shiny bob, and the 'barely there' make-up that told you she was serious rather than playing up her feminine charms.

She looked the part. He knew that she could certainly do the part; Matt had said several times that Lydia quietly picked up details other people missed.

But something in her dark eyes had told him that it wasn't who she was.

She'd even said it herself: *I don't want to be a lawyer any more.*

Ha. He knew that crossroads well. The point in your life when you wondered if you'd wasted years doing something you hadn't really wanted to do all along—something you just didn't want to do any more. The point in your life where you wondered just what it was that you really, really wanted.

And he stood by his own advice. The way forward was to give yourself a new challenge. Something to strive for. Something to help you ignore the questions.

He dismissed the thought that he hadn't found his own challenge yet. Or that he was filling his hours with a ridiculous level of work so he didn't have to think about what he really wanted from life—and how far it was from what he could actually have.

Jake shook himself and went back to poring over a set of figures. But then his email pinged: his PA had organised the flights and booked the accommodation.

Really, he should ask Ingrid to email the details to Lydia.

Then again, he still needed to brief her about the deal in Oslo.

It was something he could do perfectly adequately—and probably more quickly—by email. Or by sending Ingrid over to Lydia with the file. But somehow he found himself with the file in his hand, striding towards the legal department.

Lydia looked up from her desk as he walked into the open-plan office.

'You might want to read this before tomorrow,' he said, handing her the file. 'It's the background to the deal I'm setting up with Nils Pedersen's company in Oslo. Call me if you have any questions. I'll leave my mobile switched on this evening.'

'Noted,' she said coolly, and he knew she wouldn't call him.

He should go back to his own desk. Right now. Not linger and try to work out what that soft perfume was. Not wonder if her mouth was as soft as it looked.

'Did you manage to move your meetings?'

She nodded. 'No problem.'

'And you've spoken to Matt?'

'Via his wife, yes. He says it's OK for me to take next week off because he'll be back then.'

'Good. I'll see you at the airport at half-past nine tomorrow.'

'Nine-thirty it is.'

She was in brisk, professional lawyer mode. Efficient and quiet. Though he had a feeling that she was wearing a mask as smooth as his own. What would make her light up from the inside? he wondered.

Realising where his thoughts were going, he shook himself mentally. No. He didn't get involved nowadays. The one constant in his life was work, and he had no intentions of messing that up by having an affair with someone in the office

Besides, Lydia Sheridan wasn't the type who'd

have a temporary fling, and that was all he could offer. Jakob Andersen, heir to a shipping dynasty and CEO of Andersen Marine, couldn't offer a woman a future. Couldn't offer her anything other than wealth.

And that wasn't nearly enough.

CHAPTER TWO

WHEN Lydia walked into the departure lounge at twenty-five past nine, the next morning, Jake was already there, sitting on a chair with his right ankle resting on his left knee to make a temporary desk and a sheaf of papers cradled on his lap. There was a pen in his right hand and a mobile phone in his left, and he looked completely in command of the situation.

No wonder he was drawing admiring glances from every single female in the vicinity. That aura of confidence was incredibly sexy.

Add the fact that he had the most beautiful mouth, and...

Lydia shook herself, horrified to find herself actually fantasising about walking up to Jake and kissing him stupid. Apart from the fact that he was her boss, and therefore off limits, she'd steered clear of serious relationships since she was twenty.

Ever since she'd dated the unsuitable artist she'd overheard her father buying off.

Her disillusionment had been total. Before that

fateful afternoon, she'd seriously considered dropping out of university and following her heart, despite the fact that she'd known she'd be disappointing her parents. Because it would have meant being with the man she loved and making a living out of doing what she really wanted to do. It hadn't mattered that she and Robbie would have been practically penniless; she'd known they'd work it out, somehow, because they were a team. She'd been so sure that Robbie had loved her just as much as she had loved him.

Until she'd overheard that conversation.

And realised that Robbie hadn't hesitated even for a second before taking her father's cheque.

He'd broken up with her later that evening—just as he'd promised her father he would. He'd looked her straight in the eye and told her he was sorry, but he'd fallen in love with someone else—and she knew damn well he hadn't.

It had been a some*thing*, not a some*one*.

Money.

She dragged in a breath. That was then. This was now. But she hadn't quite let herself trust anyone since. For the year and a half after Robbie, she'd taken refuge in her studies, working hard to make sure she graduated with first-class honours and had people falling over themselves to offer her a training contract. Sure, she'd dated a few men since she left university—if she hadn't, she knew that her best friend, Emma, would have insisted on matchmaking—but she'd always kept things casual, never accepting more than half a dozen dates before saying gently that she thought they'd be better off as friends.

When was the last time she'd felt a pull of attraction like this? An urge to cup someone's face between her hands and lower her mouth to his and kiss him until they were both breathless, regardless of the fact that they were in a public place?

She couldn't remember.

But what she did know was that Jakob Anderson was definitely Mr Wrong. He was her boss. So there couldn't be a future in this.

As for the fact that she was planning huge changes in her life, changes that meant he wouldn't be her boss for much longer…Well, those changes also meant she wouldn't have time for anything else in her life. So it was pointless starting anything.

She lifted her chin, pinned a smile to her face that she didn't quite feel, and went over to sit beside him.

He acknowledged her with a nod and a brief waggle of his fingers, wrapped up his call, and turned to her. 'Good morning, Lydia.'

'Good morning.'

He glanced at his watch. 'Thanks for being punctual.' He smiled at her and she was suddenly glad she was sitting down as her knees actually went weak.

Stupid, stupid, *stupid*.

He scrutinised her boots. 'Are they waterproof?'

'They're leather.'

'And they'll be ruined within a day.' He flapped a dismissive hand. 'Never mind, we'll get you something at the airport when we land. At least your coat is suitable.'

'And it's definitely windproof.'

He tipped his head slightly to one side. 'And you know that, how?'

'My best friend nagged me into doing a sponsored walk coast to coast with her. Let's just say the north of England can be a bit windy. And wet.' She raised an eyebrow. 'Are you sure that you really need a lawyer with you? You seem to be quite good at grilling people.'

He laughed. 'Force of habit. I apologise. Do you want a coffee?'

'Do I have time to get one before our flight?'

He surprised her by scooping up his papers and putting them in his briefcase. 'Stay put and I'll get them—what do you want?'

'Latte, if they have it, please. Otherwise, just ordinary coffee with milk, no sugar. But, hang on, shouldn't I be getting these?'

Jake stood up. 'Why?'

'Because you're the head of the company, and technically I'm your junior.'

'You're my *colleague*,' he corrected, 'so we'll take it in turns to fetch coffee.' His tone brooked no argument. 'Do you want anything to eat?'

'Thanks for the offer, but no. I'm fine.'

She watched him walk away, his movements easy and graceful and incredibly sexy, and her fingers itched to sketch him.

To touch him.

Down, girl, she warned her libido silently. Wrong time, wrong place, wrong man.

He returned with coffee and gingerbread. 'It was fresh out of the oven. I'm prepared to share, but I won't argue if you refuse.'

'Your weakness?' she guessed.

'Blame it on memories of Saturday mornings in my Norwegian grandmother's kitchen.' He grinned, suddenly looking younger, and her heart skipped a beat. Jakob Andersen in work mode was gorgeous enough. In play mode, he was breathtaking.

His fingers brushed against hers as he handed her the coffee, sending a shiver of desire down her spine. She hoped he hadn't noticed; the last thing she needed now was complications.

One last job. That was what they'd agreed. And then she could resign and get on with the life she really wanted to lead.

'Do you mind if I…?' He fished his phone from his inside pocket.

'Sure. I have stuff to be getting on with, too.' Emails of her own to check on her BlackBerry.

'Fine. Help yourself to gingerbread.'

She didn't dare. Just in case she reached for the

bag at the same time as him, and their fingers ended up tangling, and she ended up blurting out the crazy ideas in her head.

This really wasn't on. For all she knew, Jake was already committed elsewhere, and the last thing they needed was an embarrassing situation just before they left the country to work together for a few days.

An insidious voice in her head reminded her that Jakob Andersen worked the kind of hours that few women would put up with, so he was probably single.

But she refused to listen. As far as she was concerned, he was off limits and staying that way.

Lydia had just about got herself under control by the time they checked in and boarded the plane. Jake was busy reading through paperwork; she knew she ought to do the same, but he'd given her the window seat and the pattern of clouds was irresistible. A glance told her that Jake was totally absorbed in what he was doing, so she took out the sketchpad and tin of pencils she always carried in her handbag, and began sketching. She worked swiftly, her pencil skimming the page.

And then she realised what she was sketching. Not the clouds: a picture in her mind's eye.

Jake.

Flushing, she closed her sketchbook and stuffed it back into her handbag. Better to concentrate on her paperwork. She opened her file, and forced herself to focus on the words in front of her.

* * *

Jake was aware of the sudden flush on Lydia's cheeks. What had happened to make her colour rise like that?

He was horribly aware that he'd like to see her skin bloom with colour in a completely different situation. One where her breathing would be ragged and her eyes would be wide with desire and her mouth would be parted and...

No.

Apart from the fact that he never dated anyone who worked for him—in his view, mixing work and relationships always ended in a mess—thoughts like these were completely inappropriate. For all he knew, Lydia was in a serious, committed relationship. There were no rings on her left hand, but that meant nothing.

Though he had heard Tim refer to her as the ice queen, as if she never dated.

The ice queen. Ha. More proof that the junior lawyer still had a lot of growing up to do. Just by looking at her, Jake could tell there was nothing icy about Lydia Sheridan. Her mouth had a sensual curve that would make any man want to reach over and touch.

Taste.

And right now he was beginning to wish that he'd brought Tim with him instead of Lydia. Because Lydia was the first woman who'd tempted him since Grace—and he wasn't sure how long he'd be able to resist.

* * *

Two hours later, the plane landed and they disembarked. It was raining, and Lydia was glad of her coat as they hurried across to the terminal.

'There's a saying in Norway: God made the country so beautiful, he must wash it every day,' Jake said, as if reading her mind. 'Oslo's beautiful at night, when all the lights reflect on the wet ground.'

She could imagine it. 'I was expecting it to be darker than this.'

'The polar nights, you mean?' He shook his head. 'We're in the south of the country, so at this time of year there are six hours of sunlight—it's not that much different from London. Dusk and dawn are a bit longer, maybe. Further north it's twilight, but it's still light enough to read by at midday.'

'Takk,' she said.

He looked at her in surprise. 'I thought you said you didn't speak Norwegian?'

'I learned a couple of phrases last night. To be polite.'

He gave her an approving smile. 'Good thinking. That'll go down well at Pedersen's. And if you want me to teach you…'

She completely missed the rest of his sentence. Because for a moment she could imagine him teaching her something, and rewarding her with a kiss. That beautiful, beautiful mouth lowering towards hers, teasing her and tasting her and arousing her until…

'Lydia?'

'Sorry. I was distracted by the scenery,' she said. It wasn't a total fib. Just that the pictures happened to be in her head, not outside. 'You were saying?'

'You're happy with the agenda?'

'It's fine. No questions.'

'Good. Oh, and keep a note of any calls you make to England from here. Andersen's will reimburse you.'

'Why would I call England?' she asked, mystified.

'Your family. To let them know you've arrived safely,' he suggested.

It hadn't occurred to her. She hadn't even told her parents that she'd be out of the country; the gulf between them had widened over the years so that she spoke to them maybe once a fortnight, and saw them even less.

Though she had told her godmother and her best friend that she'd be away. She'd promised to send postcards and take lots of photographs, especially of the Northern Lights.

'I'll call them later,' she prevaricated, not wanting to admit how difficult things were between her and her parents. 'My father will be in court at this time of day, and my mother will be in a briefing meeting.' And even if they weren't, they'd be too busy to talk to her.

'Then, if you'll excuse me?' he asked.

Jake was calling his parents?

Now that she hadn't expected.

He tapped a button on his phone. 'Mum? Yes, it's Jake. We're at Oslo Airport, safe and sound, so you can stop worrying now.' He smiled, his eyes crinkling at the corner. 'OK. Since Dad's on the golf course, you can tell him for me. I'll call you tonight.' His smile broadened. 'I love you, too.'

When had she last said, 'I love you,' to her parents? Then again, when had they last said it to her?

Jake's ease with his family unsettled Lydia. Particularly when his next call was conducted in Norwegian—and he had the same sweet, loving smile on his face when he said, *'Jeg er glad i deg.'* She didn't need a translation. This was obviously the Norwegian side of his family, and he was close to them, too.

He glanced at his watch as he put his phone away. 'Our meeting's at three, Norwegian time,' he said. 'Which means we have an hour and a half. It's going to be quickest for us to buy your boots here, then catch the shuttle train to the hotel—it'll take twice as long to get there by taxi. We'll have just about enough time to check in and unpack before we go to the office.'

'I don't need boots. These are fine,' Lydia protested.

He raised an eyebrow. 'You've been to Norway before?'

'No,' she admitted.

'Then perhaps you'll agree that I'm in a better position to judge. You do have shoes to change into, in the office?' he checked.

'Yes.'

'Good. That makes it easier.' Once they'd collected their luggage and gone through passport control, Jake ushered her over to the shopping area, asked her shoe size, then spoke in rapid Norwegian. With brisk efficiency, the assistant brought her three different styles of boots, and when she'd chosen the ones that fitted best her own boots were wrapped up and Jake had paid before she could stop him.

'I'm quite capable of paying for my own boots,' she said as they left the shop.

'I know, but it's quicker this way. We'll sort it out later,' he said.

The train took about twenty minutes and their hotel was only a couple of minutes' walk away from the station. 'Wow,' she said at her first glimpse of the sheer glass tower, silver against the grey sky. 'That's gorgeous.'

'It looks even better when the sky's blue,' he said. 'I had Ingrid book rooms for us on the thirtieth floor. The views are fantastic.'

He'd understated it, she thought when she unlocked her room and saw the fjord spreading out below. Instead of unpacking, she spent her time just drinking in the view. This was definitely something she'd sketch, later.

She heard a knock at the door, and glanced at her watch. They needed to be going. Quickly, she slipped her shoes into her briefcase, gathered up her coat and handbag and opened the door. 'Sorry. I was admiring the view.'

'Hopefully we'll have time for me to show you a bit of the city in the evenings. If it dries up,' he said with a smile. 'It's not far to Nils's office, but it's bucketing down outside so I've booked us a taxi.'

Nils Pedersen's office was in Aker Brygge Wharf. 'It used to be a shipyard,' Jake explained on the way there, 'but it's been developed as a business and tourist centre. It's really pretty in the summer. My grandfather says that when he was a boy, in the winter the fjord would freeze and they'd make roads with sledges on the ice, and as spring came they'd cut channels in the ice. Of course, winters are milder now.'

'You really love Norway, don't you?' she asked.

'Of course. It's my home, where my father's family live.' He smiled. 'I guess I'm greedy, because England's home, too. My mother's English.'

At the office, they were shown into a conference room; Jake introduced Lydia to the people who were already sitting at the table.

'God ettermiddag,' she said, and her effort was rewarded with a beaming smile from everyone who shook her hand.

She wasn't surprised that the meeting was brisk and efficient, cutting through the personal niceties and sticking strictly to business—she could definitely see where Jake got that from. But when the meeting ended at four-thirty, she raised an eyebrow.

'Normal office hours in Norway are eight till four,' he explained as they left. 'Pedersen's have already accommodated us by working later tonight. And dinner's early in Norway, too—we eat at six rather than eight. I hope you don't mind, but I've accepted Nils's invitation to dine with him and his family tonight.'

'No worries. I wasn't expecting you to look after me every minute of the day. I'll order something from room service.'

'That isn't what I meant. The invitation's for both of us,' he said gently. 'I wouldn't be selfish enough to abandon you in a country you'd never been to before.'

'Oh.' She flushed. 'Well, just let me know the dress code. And any points of etiquette that aren't the same as in England.'

'Smart casual, nothing too glittery. All you need to remember is that we won't talk business tonight—in Norway, we keep business and home separate. Oh, and take your shoes off at the door. Otherwise, just be yourself.' He smiled. 'Nils was impressed that you'd taken the trouble to learn some Norwegian—especially when I told him I'd only drafted you in yesterday. Elisabet—his wife— speaks English, so there will be no problem tonight.'

They went back to the hotel via the main shopping street, where Jake chose a good bottle of white wine and some bright pink gerberas.

'Do Nils and Elisabet have children?' she asked.

'Yes, a boy and a girl. They're both at nursery.'

'We should take them something, too. Could I buy them some art stuff?'

Jake looked surprised for a moment, then nodded. 'Better than taking them sweets. If you think they'll like them, that is.'

'My best friend's a primary school teacher. According to her, all kids love art stuff.'

'I wouldn't know.'

Jake's face was completely unreadable, but Lydia had the distinct feeling that she'd just trampled over a sore spot. And it was pretty fair to assume now that Jake was definitely single with no kids. Or maybe that was it: he was divorced, and his ex had made access to his children impossible—maybe by moving away.

Not that it was any of her business.

But she made a mental note to be tactful in future.

Jake took her to a toyshop and let her choose various craft gifts, which she insisted on paying for. 'I'm a guest, too, and, as you've already bought wine and flowers, I'm buying these. No arguments.'

He inclined his head and allowed her to pay.

Back at the hotel, Lydia had enough time to shower and change into a simple black dress and low-heeled court shoes before the taxi arrived.

'You look nice,' Jake said approvingly when she opened the door to him.

'Thank you. So do you.' Though that was an

understatement. His blue shirt really brought out
the colour of his eyes. He'd clearly just shaved, too,
and for a mad moment she found her hand lifting to
touch his face, feel how soft his skin was.

She just about managed to stop herself, and was
glad she had when he said coolly, 'The taxi should
be waiting for us downstairs.'

They arrived at the Pedersens' at two minutes to
six, and Nils welcomed them warmly, introducing
them to his wife Elisabet. The two children peeped
shyly from behind Elisabet's skirts.

Jake crouched down to their level and held out
his hand, speaking gently in Norwegian, and the
little boy shook his hand solemnly, followed by his
little sister.

Lydia followed his lead. 'Hello,' she said.
'*Beklager*, I don't speak much Norwegian. I'm
English.'

Elisabet translated rapidly for the children, then
smiled at Lydia. 'This is Morten.'

'Hello,' the little boy said, and shook her hand.

'And this is Kristin.'

'Hello,' the little girl said shyly, copying her brother.

Jake straightened up. 'Thank you for inviting us
over. It's very kind of you,' he said, handing the
flowers to Elisabet and the wine to Nils.

'And we thought the children might like these,'
Lydia said, indicating the bag she was carrying, 'but
if I give them to you, Mrs Pedersen, you can let the

children have them at a better time. It's pencils and stickers and paper, that sort of thing.'

'Call me Elisabet. And *tusen takk* for the gift— thank you so much. How lovely. They adore drawing,' Elisabet said with a smile. 'They're off to bed soon, but they'd enjoy making a picture now, if you'd like to give them the presents yourself?'

Lydia glanced at Jake, who nodded and said something swiftly in the children's own language.

Shyly, Morten accepted the bag; and although Lydia couldn't understand more than *takk* from the little boy's excited babble, she could see the pleasure on both children's faces.

'Come through. I will get you a drink,' Nils said.

'Is there anything I can do to help?' Lydia asked.

'You can join me in the kitchen, if you like.' Elisabet scooped up her daughter. 'Where I can finish preparing dinner and keep an eye on these two.'

'You can probably get Lydia to draw them something,' Jake said. 'She's good at art.'

Lydia's heart skipped a beat. How did he know? Had he seen her sketching on the plane? She only hoped that he'd seen her sketches of the clouds, not the portrait she'd drawn of him. A quick glance at his face left her none the wiser; his expression was completely unreadable.

'Come through,' Elisabet said, leading the way to the kitchen. She helped Kristin onto a stool by the breakfast bar and watched as Morten climbed up next to her; within seconds, the children had the pencils and paper spread across the work surface and were busy drawing patterns.

'*Takk* for translating for me,' Lydia said. 'I'm sorry, I only knew I was coming to Norway yesterday afternoon. I haven't had time to learn more than please, thank you and hello.'

'It's good that you've learned that much,' Elisabet said. 'Though most Norwegians speak English.'

'Are those the children's drawings from school?' She gestured to the pictures held on the fridge with magnets. 'They're very good.'

'Thank you. And Jake said you're good at art?'

'I sketch a bit,' Lydia said diffidently. 'Maybe I could teach the children to draw something? A cat for Morten and a butterfly for Kristin to colour, maybe?'

'That would be lovely.' Elisabet translated rapidly for the children, who beamed. 'I think that's a yes,' she said with a smile.

'Shouldn't I help you with something, first?' Lydia asked.

'You already are. You're keeping the children happy,' Elisabet said.

Lydia took a piece of paper, then drew the outline of a butterfly for Kristin. She picked up a pink pencil and drew a simple curved shape inside the outline, colouring it in, then offered the pencil to the little girl. Kristin took it shyly, and drew a shape herself; once Lydia was sure that the little girl was happy, she showed Morten how to draw a simple outline of a cat. The little boy copied it haltingly.

'Very good,' she said, clapping.

He beamed at her, and drew a second cat, this time with more confidence, then a third; he called out to his mother, who came to inspect it and praised him.

'I envy you. I'm not so good at art—I can barely draw a straight line with a ruler,' Elisabet confessed. 'I hate it if they sign me up to do arty things for *Julemessa*—the nursery fundraising Christmas fair.'

'But you,' Lydia said, gesturing to the beautiful ring cake filled with fruit and cream that stood on the worktop, 'can make wonderful cakes. Which I can't. They go flat as a pancake—so I cheat and buy them at the baker's.'

'Just like I cheat and make Nils do the painting,' Elisabet confided with a smile.

'Would you like me to sketch the children for you?' Lydia asked.

'Very much,' Elisabet said.

Lydia needed no second invitation. She took her pencils and sketchbook from her handbag, and began to draw.

Jake had followed Nils into the kitchen from the door at the other end of the room, and stood there in silence, watching Lydia as she sketched; she looked completely at home, chatting to Elisabet and stopping what she was doing every so often to help one of the children.

He could imagine her like that with children of her own, kind and patient and supportive, and the hollow in his stomach filled with bile. Yet another reason why he had no right to start any kind of relationship with Lydia: children were absolutely not on his agenda, not any more.

And how hard it was, to smile and be polite and pretend that everything was just fine. Still, he ought to be used to it, by now. He'd managed it before. He'd manage it tonight. He forced himself to walk casually over towards Lydia and glanced over her shoulder.

He'd thought her cloud pictures on the plane were good, but these were fabulous. With a few deft strokes of her pencil, she'd really captured both children: Kristin, concentrating on her butterfly, and Morten's expression as it changed from effort to triumph as he realised he'd managed to draw a cat just the way she'd taught him.

'You're very talented.'

'Thank you.'

Though Jake noticed that she kept a tight hold of her sketchbook as she removed the pages with the sketches of the children, then stuffed it back in her handbag without offering to let anyone look through it. So she was as unconfident about her talent as she was about her work as a lawyer? Someone must really have done a number on her, in the past.

Nils and Elisabet were both delighted with the sketches. Nils took the children up to bed and read them a story, while Elisabeth ushered them into the dining room and brought the first course in.

Dinner was fine: good food and good conversation, with Nils and Elisabet suggesting places in Oslo that Lydia really ought to see before she returned to England. The opera house, a night-time walk along the Akerselva river, the sculptures in Vigeland park and the Viking ships in the museum.

Lydia seemed to blossom in their company, opening up about her favourite places to sketch in London. And Jake realised just how pretty she was: her dark eyes sparkled, her face was animated, and the candlelight brought out the copper and gold lights in her hair.

He had to force himself to stop staring at her mouth.

And every so often he caught her eye and saw the colour bloom on her cheeks.

She worked for him, he reminded himself. And he wasn't in a position to offer her anything more than a fling. He needed to get himself back under control.

And yet…he'd noticed that she was looking at him, too.

So he wasn't alone in this crazy attraction. Maybe she was wondering the same thing as he was. What it would be like to touch her skin; how it would feel to kiss her.

At the end of the evening, he thanked Nils and

Elisabet for their hospitality, but when he climbed into the taxi beside Lydia he fell silent.

It would be so easy to ask her…

But that would be taking unfair advantage of the situation. Plus, if he'd misread the signs, it would be way too awkward at work tomorrow. This deal was too important to jeopardise.

And for the life of him he couldn't think of a neutral topic of conversation. All he could think of was how much he wanted to cradle that beautiful heart-shaped face in his hands and touch his mouth to hers, coax her into responding. A sweet, slow kiss that would deepen and deepen and end up with his body driving into hers.

He could hardly say that, could he?

'Did I do something wrong?' Lydia asked eventually.

'Wrong?' He didn't follow.

'You're a bit, um, quiet.' She dragged in a breath. 'Look, if I made a faux pas tonight, I'd appreciate knowing what it was, so I don't repeat it.'

'No, you're fine—it's not you.' It was definitely him. Not that he intended to tell her what was in his head. 'I guess I'm a bit tired.' He lifted one shoulder. 'Every time my mother sees me, she nags me about working too hard.'

'Maybe she has a point,' Lydia said.

'I'm fine.' To his relief, the taxi arrived at the hotel. He paid the fare, then walked in to the hotel foyer with her. 'I was planning to go for a swim tomorrow morning before breakfast in my room. We're due in the office at eight, so I'll call for you at quarter to.'

He didn't quite catch her expression before she masked it, and after he'd seen her safely to her room and opened his own door, he was still thinking about it. Had it been relief that he didn't expect her to spend every waking minute of the day with him?

Or had it been disappointment?

'Get a grip,' he told himself crossly, and headed for a cold shower. Hopefully the temperature would knock some sense back into his head.

CHAPTER THREE

AFTER two days of working closely with Lydia, Jake was going quietly crazy. He managed to keep his mind focused on work in the office; but when they were back at the hotel nothing could get her out of his mind. Cold showers, long swims, workouts in the hotel gym... Nothing worked.

It was even worse when Lydia was sitting next to him at the table in the sitting room of his suite, working her way through the contract they were hammering out with Nils. All he could think about was leaning across to kiss her—and the fact that his bedroom was only a few steps away.

On the Friday night, Lydia was talking him through the document. Jake was hardly aware of what she was saying; he couldn't take his eyes off her mouth. And because she wore hardly any make-up, her lips were their natural shape and colour: a soft blush rose, with a natural pout.

All he could think about was how much he wanted to taste her.

How much he wanted to plunder.

How much he wanted that gorgeous mouth kissing him back, demanding everything he was prepared to give and offering just as much back.

'Jake? Is that OK with you?'

'Uh. Yeah. You're absolutely right.' Actually, he didn't have a clue what Lydia had just said, but he'd seen her work firsthand over the last couple of days. She was meticulous, so he had absolute confidence in her judgement.

And he went back to watching her mouth. Keeping himself in check—just—but still wondering.

Until the moment he let his gaze flicker up to her eyes and realised that she was staring at him, too. That she was looking at *his* mouth.

Was she wondering what it would feel like if…?

No. He had to be sensible about this.

He dragged his attention back to the contract. Managed to discuss it with her as if he were totally focused on business.

But then they both reached for the same piece of paper at the same time, and their fingers brushed by accident. It felt as if he'd been hit by lightning. Jake's whole body quivered, and his control finally snapped; he twisted round to face Lydia, slid his hands into her hair, and brushed his mouth against hers.

The lightest, sweetest, gentlest kiss.

His lips tingled where they'd touched hers, and

he was about to kiss her again more thoroughly when his common sense kicked in.

What the hell was he doing? Apart from the fact that he was setting himself up for being sued for sexual harassment, he'd promised himself that he wouldn't give in to his body's urging. He'd promised himself that he'd be sensible about this, that he'd ignore the attraction.

He was about to loosen his hands, move away and apologise, when he felt a soft kiss pressed against his mouth.

Lydia was kissing him back.

Jake's control splintered again, and he responded, nibbling her lower lip until her mouth opened, letting him deepen the kiss and explore her mouth more intimately. His hands glided down her back to her waist; right now, he needed to touch as well as taste. He untucked her shirt from the waistband of her skirt and slid his fingers underneath the cotton so he could splay his palms against her back. Her skin was warm and smooth and soft, and it made him want to explore further. He moved his fingertips in tiny circles against her skin, and she murmured something against his mouth.

The tiny sound broke the spell and he stopped, pulling away from her and staring at her, aghast. Lydia—the cool, calm lawyer he'd worked with all week—looked completely dishevelled. And it was all his fault.

Ah, hell. What had he been thinking?

'I'm sorry, Lydia,' he said. 'I shouldn't have done that.'

Her eyes were wide and worried as she looked back at him, but she didn't say a word.

He raked a hand through his hair and stared at the table. 'I apologise. I can assure you that I don't normally leap on my colleagues like that— and it certainly wasn't the reason why I brought you to Norway.'

'I know.'

There was the tiniest, tiniest quiver in her voice, which made him look at her. Her mouth was lush and reddened with his kisses; he just about managed to drag his gaze to her eyes, and then he realised that she was staring at his mouth again, too.

So it really wasn't just him. She wanted this, too.

He needed to talk to her about this. To do the honourable thing—explain that he couldn't offer her any more than a fling.

But then she reached up with a shy smile. Pressed the flat of her palm to his cheek, and rubbed the pad of her thumb along his lower lip. Automatically, his mouth opened; he drew her thumb into his mouth and sucked. Hard. Her pupils grew huge and her mouth parted, and Jake was lost.

He released her thumb, cupped her face with both hands and lowered his mouth to hers again. She tasted like heaven; her mouth was warm and sweet and giving, and he just couldn't get enough. He wanted everything she was offering, and more.

Kissing her made his head spin, and the next thing he knew they were standing by his bed. He had absolutely no idea whether they'd walked there or whether he'd gone caveman and carried her there.

But what he did know was that this was absolutely mutual. Because she'd untucked his shirt and her hands were underneath the soft cotton, her fingertips teasing her skin just as he'd teased hers earlier.

His blood felt as though it were fizzing in his veins, her touch made him so hot.

'If you want me to stop,' he said, his voice shaking slightly, 'you need to tell me now.'

'Don't stop.' Her voice was practically a whisper, and as quivery as his own, and her pupils were enormous. She was just as turned on as he was, needed the release just as much as he did. She was with him all the way. So he could do exactly what he'd wanted to do for *days*.

He undid the buttons of her shirt, taking it slowly and stroking tiny circles on her skin with the tips of his fingers as he revealed it. He could see from the way her nipples hardened, visible through the cream lace of her bra, that she liked it. Good. Because he loved the warmth and softness of her skin beneath his hands, the way her body responded to his touch.

He bent his head to kiss the curve of her neck, tracing a path of kisses along her collarbones and lingering in the hollows. That soft floral scent he'd noticed back in London, warm and sweet… 'You smell gorgeous,' he murmured. 'What is it?'

'Gardenia.'

'It's fabulous.' Tomorrow, he'd buy her more. He'd run a deep, foamy bath scented with the stuff, and make love with her in it. He undid the buttons at her wrists, then slid her shirt from her shoulders. He traced the lacy edge of her bra, then rubbed the pad of his thumb against her hardened nipples; she dragged in a breath and tipped her head back, offering her throat to him.

'Jake. You're driving me crazy,' she whispered.

'You're driving me crazy, too. I want to touch you, Lydia. See you.' He paused. '*Taste* you.'

'Yes.' The word was almost a hiss of pleasure, and colour bloomed in her cheeks. Colour that he was going to make, oh, so much more intense when he made love with her. And they were both going to enjoy every second of it.

'I need to touch you, too,' she whispered.

Within limits.

He'd stop her before it got…complicated.

He slid one bra strap off her shoulder and kissed the bare skin. 'I'm in your hands, *min kjære*.'

She undid the buttons of his shirt, her fingers hesitant at first and then more confident; once she'd bared his chest, she splayed her fingers across it. 'You're perfect.'

He smiled wryly. 'And you're good for my ego.'

Her hands drifted lower, over his abdomen, and he felt a kick of excitement as she undid his belt.

Funny, it was like being a teenager again. The sense of urgency, the need, the feeling that he was somehow stepping into the unknown. He couldn't remember the last time he'd felt like that.

Certainly not with Grace.

But it was pointless feeling bitter about it. Practically anyone would've done the same, in his ex-fiancée's position. And she'd done him a favour, really—she'd saved him from future heartache, because he wasn't going to let anyone into his heart again. Wasn't going to let anyone close enough to reject him the way Grace had.

This was one night out of time.

Getting the mutual attraction out of their systems.

Tomorrow, maybe everything would be back to normal and he could be sensible again. Tonight, he was going to give in to the need that was driving him crazy, and lose himself in Lydia.

He quivered as she undid the button of his trousers, lowered the zip infinitely slowly and trailed one fingertip along his erection through the soft cotton of his underpants.

What it would feel like, to be skin to skin with her...

But she was getting a little too close for comfort. Gently, he locked his hand round hers. Stopped her. 'I'd rather you didn't.'

She flushed. 'I'm sorry. I'm not usually this…'

She broke off, but he could guess the rest. *Uninhibited. Reckless.*

Now she was embarrassed, clearly believing that he thought she was easy.

Oh, hell. He hadn't thought that she might take it that way; he'd just wanted to avoid an awkward explanation. 'It's not that, *min kjære.*' He fumbled for the right words to reassure her. 'You're delightful.'

She said nothing, but her eyes were so expressive. *Really?*

Someone had obviously hurt her very, very badly. Hacked her confidence away.

And he was a bastard to take advantage of her like this. He really ought to stop.

Yet, if he stopped now, he knew they'd both feel bad. Awkward, embarrassed and frustrated. And he wanted to make Lydia feel good. He wanted to see her eyes go hazy with desire and her body arching against his.

So he dropped a sweet, reassuring kiss on her mouth. 'It's not you, *elskling.* Only…' He'd tell her the truth. Just not the whole truth. 'It's been a while for me, and I find your touch incredibly arousing. If you touch me now, I won't be able to make it good for you.'

The wariness in her eyes vanished, to his relief, and he caught her lower lip gently between his.

'And I want to make it good for you, Lydia. I want to blow your mind.'

'You're doing pretty well so far,' she said shakily.

He undid the zip of her skirt and eased the material over her hips so it fell to the floor; then he dropped to his knees before her and rolled her tights slowly downwards. As he stroked her inner thighs, she shivered. Good. Because he needed her too turned on to think straight and use that clever lawyer's mind when they were finally skin to skin. He stroked the sensitive spot at the back of her knee, then drew her tights down over her calves, her ankles. Her skin was so soft; he didn't think he'd ever be able to stop touching her.

He pressed his mouth against her abdomen and kissed his way up to her ribcage, breathing in her scent and loving it. Deftly, he unclipped her bra, letting it drop to the floor while he cupped her breasts. 'Oh. Now this, I *really* like.' He rubbed the pads of his thumbs over her nipples, enjoying her little gasp of response. 'Lydia Sheridan, you're utterly gorgeous, and right now I feel like a kid in a sweetshop. I want to look, to touch, I want everything.'

He rose to his feet, kicked off his shoes and removed his trousers and socks, then lifted her onto the bed, laying her back against the pillows.

'You're absolutely sure you don't want me to stop?' he checked, wanting to make it clear that he wasn't taking her for granted.

'If you don't touch me in the next nanosecond,

I'm going to go completely insane.' Her voice had grown deeper, huskier, with arousal.

'Good,' he said, and knelt between her parted thighs. He teased one nipple with his lips and tongue.

'Oh, yes, Jake,' she whispered, sliding her hands into his hair and urging him on. 'Yes.'

He teased her other nipple, then kissed his way down her abdomen. When he slid one finger underneath the edge of her knickers, she quivered and arched against him, tilting her hips to give him the access he wanted. Slowly, looking straight into her eyes, he pushed one finger inside her. She felt like hot, wet silk wrapped round him. Glorious. But it wasn't enough. He wanted to see her shatter in climax, her mouth parted and her eyes unfocused with pleasure. He wanted to know that his touch could turn this clever, capable woman to mush.

And he wanted her to do exactly the same to him.

He moved his thumb to tease her clitoris, and she dragged in a breath.

'Don't tease, Jake.'

'No teasing, *min kjære*.' But he needed her right on the edge before he removed the rest of his clothes. Too caught up in the moment to think. Because, despite the surgeon's skill, he was sure that it was obvious.

And he knew that if Lydia noticed, she'd ask. Tactfully, but she'd definitely ask.

'Lift up for me,' he said softly. She did so, and he swiftly removed her knickers, abandoning them over the side of the bed.

Lydia had never had hot sex with a man she wasn't even officially dating. This was way, way out of character for her.

And she didn't regret a single second of it.

Because Jakob Andersen was gorgeous. His body was firm and toned, his skin was soft, and he knew exactly how to use his mouth and his hands to give her maximum pleasure. How to stoke her desire higher and higher until she was burning.

He kissed the hollows of her ankles, and as his lips moved slowly upwards her pulse quickened. She realised exactly what he had in mind—and, oh, she wanted it.

Desperately.

She could feel the heat of his breath against her inner thighs; she gripped the pillow and held on for dear life as she finally felt the touch of his mouth against her sex, the long, slow stroke of his tongue exploring and teasing and stoking her desire.

'Oh, yes. Jake. Please, *yes*.' She hardly even recognised the voice coming from her mouth, it was so guttural and deep. And it didn't matter that she was begging shamelessly, because she knew that later she'd have him in exactly the same state—completely given over to pleasure and wanting more. This was mutual.

'Please,' she whispered. 'I need you. Inside me. Now.'

Jake knew he had her exactly where he wanted her: at the point where she wasn't going to ask questions. Where her need for him was so great, she'd accept him exactly as he was.

He climbed off the bed and grabbed his wallet from his trousers. The condom in there was so old, it was probably out of date. But in the circumstances, that didn't matter. There was no real need for protection: he could tell that Lydia didn't make a habit of sleeping around, and neither did he. And, more to the point, he couldn't make her pregnant. Not without the help of a laboratory and an army of doctors—and she'd be the one who'd have to go through the mill.

But he didn't want to explain all that. To see the pity in her eyes.

Not yet.

So he'd play this as if everything were completely normal.

Lydia closed her eyes, focusing on the moment when Jake would be kneeling back between her thighs. She heard the sound of foil ripping, and then the mattress dipped again beneath his weight.

At last.

The tip of his penis nudged against her entrance; and finally, with one slow, deep thrust, he was inside her. In response, she wrapped her legs round his waist, tilting her hips and urging him deeper.

'OK?' he asked softly.

She opened her eyes and smiled at him. 'Very OK.' She almost blurted out that he was the perfect fit, but stopped herself; instead, she slid her hands into his hair, drawing his head down to hers and kissing him deeply.

It shouldn't have felt this good, not for a first time. But she'd never been in tune with anyone before, the way she was with Jake.

She could feel the pressure growing as he moved, her climax building and building and building, until she didn't think she could take any more. She gasped out his name as she hit the peak, and felt his answering shudder before he wrapped his arms round her, rolling onto his back and taking her with him so that her head was pillowed on his shoulder.

She lay against him, utterly sated; and then, gently, he moved her to the side.

'I'm just going to deal with the condom,' he said softly, and brushed a kiss against her mouth.

When he returned, she noticed that he was wearing soft grey boxer shorts. And he didn't remove them before climbing back into bed with her.

Shy?

Or regretting what they'd done?

She felt her face heating. How did you say to a man that you'd just had the best sex of your entire life with him—but it was OK, you could see it wasn't the same for him, so if he wouldn't mind looking the other way you'd get dressed and leave now?

Completely out of her depth, she closed her eyes and wished that she were a thousand miles away.

'Lydia.' He touched the back of his fingers lightly against her cheek. 'I think we need to talk.'

Uh-oh. Here it came.

Well, she was going to say it first. Salvage some of her pride. 'I'm sorry. That shouldn't have happened.'

'We both knew it would.'

What? That made her open her eyes and look at him.

'You're right. It shouldn't have happened. We're supposed to be colleagues.' He smiled wryly. 'I've already made a mess of this. I can't make it much worse, so I might as well be open with you. I can't take my eyes off you,' he admitted. 'And I think it's the same for you. Every time I've glanced at you for the last two days, you've been looking at me, too.'

Lydia flushed. 'Um. I was trying to be discreet.'

'Me, too,' he said wryly. 'I'm normally so in control. But I lost it, just now. And I think you did, as well.'

She swallowed. 'Just so you know, I'm not in the habit of—'

'—leaping into bed with someone you haven't been dating,' he finished. 'I know. I don't, either. But there's something about you that makes me… Ah, I don't know.' He raked his hand through his hair.

Lydia felt desire pulse through her again. She'd just bet he had no idea how sexy he looked with his hair all messy like that—all tough and Viking marauder.

'There isn't an easy way to say this.'

'But this was just one night and can we just forget it happened?' she suggested.

'Is that what you want?'

She couldn't read his expression at all. Surely he should be looking relieved that she was letting him off the hook so easily? Or did he want this to be the start of something else?

This was crazy.

She knew what she ought to say. Yes, this was just one night and we'll forget about it. But something entirely different slipped out. 'I don't know.'

'So your head's saying yes and your body's saying, you want more?' he asked.

Oh, this was bad. 'You could've warned me you're a mind-reader,' she muttered, splaying a hand over her face to hide her embarrassment.

He laughed, took her hand and raised it to his lips. Kissed the back of her hand, and kept it cradled in his own. 'I'm not. I'm just saying what I'm feeling.' He grew serious as she looked at him. 'But I need to be fair with you, Lydia. Whatever this thing is between us—and I can't explain it either—I can't offer you a future.'

'You're committed elsewhere?'

'Absolutely not.' He shook his head in emphasis. 'I'd never cheat. I've been single for a while, now. No strings, no complications. You?'

'No. There's nobody.'

'So there's no reason why we can't have a mad fling and blow each other's minds for the next few days. Well, apart from the fact that I'm your boss, and ethically that makes this completely wrong.'

But at that precise moment he couldn't give a damn about ethics.

The only thing that filled his head was the need to touch her again. To ease his body into hers. To see her eyes widen with pleasure as he brought her to climax—and feel her body tightening round his, tipping him into his own release.

'I have a suggestion.' He paused. 'You know you said you didn't want to be a lawyer any more? That you'd fallen out of love with your job?'

She lifted one shoulder. 'I'm not sure I was ever in love with it in the first place.'

He frowned. 'Then why do it? Qualifying as a lawyer means years of training. That's a lot of effort to put into something you don't actually want to do.'

'It's…' She wrinkled her nose. 'It's complicated.'

'Try me. I saw you sketching the clouds on the plane. You want to be an artist?'

'I don't want to talk about it right now.' But her fingers tightened round his, telling him that she wasn't pushing him away: she just didn't want to talk about her job.

'So you're at a crossroads.'

'Yes,' she admitted.

'Me, too.' It was something he hadn't told anyone. Not even those he was closest to. His parents, his grandparents, his best friend… Nobody. He'd barely been able to admit it to himself. Funny how it was easier to say it to someone who was almost a stranger. 'I need to decide what I want out of life.'

She stared at him in apparent surprise. 'But you're CEO of Andersen Marine. Head of your family's firm.'

'I know.' He paused, unsure how to phrase it. 'I'm just not sure that's enough for me.'

'What, you're planning world domination, next?' she asked dryly.

He laughed. 'No. I don't know what I want.' Well, he did. Though he knew he wasn't going to get it, so it was pointless wishing for it. What he needed to find was the right substitute. Something to keep him going. Until…

Well.

He didn't want to think about *that*, either.

'I have a theory that it's to do with hitting thirty this year.' Partly, anyway. In his case, there was a little more to it than that. 'When you have a milestone birthday, it makes you reassess your life and question every decision you've made so far.'

Her eyes narrowed slightly. 'How do you know I was thirty this year?'

'I looked it up in your file before we came out here.'

She gave him a wry smile. 'At least you're honest about it.'

'I'm honest about everything.' Well, almost. There were some things he tried not to think about. And that was self-preservation rather than cowardice. 'Right now, I think we're both in the same place,' he said quietly. 'We both need space, time to decide what we really want. And Norway's the perfect place to think—there's nowhere to hide. So that's my suggestion. We spend a week here. Together. And this thing between us…we can get it out of our systems.'

'You're saying we should have an affair.'

'With limits. So we know the deal right from the start.'

'An affair,' she repeated. 'For a week. A seven-night stand.'

'Put like that, it sounds tacky.' He grimaced. 'I'm trying not to be dishonourable. I can't offer you more than an affair, Lydia. I can't offer *anyone* more than that.'

'Might I ask why?'

'Tell me why you're a lawyer,' he said, 'and I'll tell you why I can't offer anything with a future.'

The corner of her mouth quirked. 'So you're suggesting an affair with counselling.'

He rolled his eyes. 'You're a lawyer, all right. No.'

'What, then?'

'Space to think, and someone to bounce ideas off.'

'And hot sex.' The words were clearly out before she could stop them, and she clapped a hand to her mouth in apparent horror. 'I didn't mean to say that.'

He couldn't help a wide smile. 'I'm very glad you did. Because I think your mind's working on the same lines as mine. And right now I've got some seriously X-rated pictures of you in my head.'

She licked her lower lip, and he almost lost control again.

'This is mad,' she whispered. 'You're my *boss.*'

'Technically. For the moment. But this doesn't have anything to do with work. This is just between you and me.' His gaze held hers. 'Equal.'

'Just so you know,' she said, 'I'm not looking for a relationship, either. It's the wrong time in my life.'

And she was proud. He'd already gathered that.

'So this is a week out of time. No strings, no re-criminations.' He wrinkled his nose in annoyance. 'That makes it sound like a business deal, and it's not. I want to spend the next week making love with you, Lydia. Touching you and tasting you until I know the feel of your skin as well as I do my own.'

She blew out a breath. 'No limits.'

Oh, there were limits, all right. Limits that meant he couldn't offer her more than a week. 'You and me. Hot sex. And we can go anywhere you like. You said you wanted to see the Northern Lights.'

'Yes.'

He loosened her hand. 'We'll need to be away from the city so there's no light pollution to get in the way. And it depends on the weather, too. But we can go north. Try to find them.' He smiled wryly. This was going to sound clichéd, but he was pretty sure that she was thinking it, too. 'And maybe try to find ourselves. Work out what we really want out of life.'

She was silent for so long that he thought she was going to be sensible and say no.

And then she looked at him. 'I don't do this sort of thing, Jake. If you're expecting some super-sexy woman, you've got the wrong one.'

Didn't she have any idea how lovely she was?

Just as she'd doubted her ability at work—and he'd seen for himself that she was good at what she did. He had a feeling that she wasn't turning him down because she didn't want to do this—rather, she was saying that she didn't think she'd live up to his expectations. 'For your information,' he said softly, 'it's been driving me crazy, this last couple of days. You wouldn't believe how many cold showers I've had to take because of you.'

'Really?' She looked surprised.

'Really.' He drew the pad of his thumb along her lower lip. 'Don't make a habit of underestimating yourself, *min kjære.*'

'I don't underestimate myself.'

'Yes, you do.' He tucked a strand of hair behind her ear. 'You just told me not to expect some supersexy woman. So clearly it hasn't occurred to you that I might find you incredibly attractive, just the way you are.'

She blew out a breath. 'If we're going to do this week, I don't want any flattery.'

'No flattery. Haven't you noticed that I can't keep my hands off you?'

She didn't answer that.

He stole a kiss. 'Don't think you have to act up to what you think my ideal lover would be. Just be yourself.'

'Be myself.' She gave him a tight smile. 'Yeah.'

CHAPTER FOUR

LYDIA masked her expression quickly, but not quickly enough. Jake had seen the misery there and it made his heart ache.

'Whoever he was, he really did a number on you.' He shifted, pulling her onto his lap and wrapping his arms round her.

'I don't know what you mean.'

'Yes, you do. But I realise you're not ready to talk about it yet.' Just as he wasn't ready to talk about bits of his own life. 'So let me ask you a question. Do you trust my judgement?'

'Your judgement?'

'My business judgement,' he clarified.

'Yes.'

'Why do you trust my judgement?' This wasn't about his ego; it was making sure that she wasn't paying lip-service to his question—and getting her to admit things, step by step.

'Because Andersen's did well under your dad, but you've raised the game and expanded the company.

And the deal you made this week was sensible underpinning for further expansion.'

'Right. So would you agree that my judgement is sound?' He knew he was hammering his line of reasoning home, but she was a lawyer. He'd work in the way that she understood. Point by point.

'Your business judgement, yes.'

'I'm the same in business as I am in person.'

'I only have your word for that,' she reminded him.

'Do you trust my word?'

'That depends where this is heading.'

He sighed. 'Spoken like a lawyer. OK, Lydia, I'm going to tell you how I see you. You hide behind your business suit, but you're all curves and your mouth has that kind of sensuality that would make any man want to yank you into his arms and kiss you.'

She scoffed. 'That's not sexy.'

'Sure, you're not the sort who wears clinging, low-cut tops and skirts that practically show the world your knickers and heels so high you can barely walk in them—but *that* really isn't sexy. It's too obvious. Tacky, even.'

She flushed.

'What's sexy,' he continued, 'is seeing this clever, quiet, capable woman across a boardroom table, and knowing that behind closed doors and in my arms I'll get to see the woman nobody else sees. Someone who's warm and sensual. Someone who's a little shy with me right now, but I hope is going to open up to me a little more and tell me exactly how and where she likes to be touched and kissed—just as she'd cut through the hype on a business deal.'

'That's your idea of sexy.'

'Uh-huh. Just so you know. I find you incredibly attractive.' He shifted slightly so she could feel his erection pressing against her. 'And, if words aren't enough, I think you can feel the effect it has on me, you sitting on my lap.'

She quivered. 'Um, yes.'

'And that's *you* causing that reaction. Not some idea of a super-sexy woman. Just you.' He kissed the hollow beneath her ear. 'So. A week out of time. You and me. Space to think and someone to bounce ideas off, with no judgements. How about it?'

'In theory it's a good idea.'

He laughed. 'That sounded like a lawyer's "but". Hit me with it.'

'I arranged my time off before we left London, but you're the CEO of the company. You can't just take time off on a whim. You've got one hell of a schedule.'

He shrugged. 'Ingrid can rearrange my appointments. I'll check my emails twice a day. And my deputy's perfectly capable of handling anything urgent—or calling Dad, if it's something really time-critical and he needs an answer right there and then.' He smiled wryly. 'Though Ingrid might faint at the idea of me actually taking a break.'

'When was your last time off?'

'A while back.'

'How long back?'

He rolled his eyes. 'Forget being a corporate lawyer. You could've been a top barrister. Nothing gets past you, does it?'

'How long back?' she repeated.

He sighed. 'My sabbatical.' Except he hadn't been on holiday, having fun. He'd been recovering from surgery. For cancer. Which was in remission right now, but there were no guarantees that it wouldn't come back.

'It's *eighteen months* since you had any time off?' She looked shocked. 'Under employment law, that's illegal.'

'It's my company. I'm hardly going to sue myself.' He shrugged. 'What about you? When was the last time you had a holiday?'

'Earlier this year. I went on the coast-to-coast walk with my best friend.'

'Forgive me for being rude, but you don't strike me as the hiking type. I see you more the sort who'd spend a week touring art galleries in a European city somewhere.'

'I am,' she said. 'But Emma and I turned thirty within three weeks of each other, and she suggested that we do something different to celebrate. Something a bit more substantial than a party, and a bit less indulgent than swanning off to Florence or Prague for a long weekend.'

He smiled. 'And she nags you about your lifestyle?'

'She gangs up on me with my godmother,' Lydia admitted ruefully. 'But if I take time off and start sketching…'

'It makes you realise what you're missing and you can't handle it,' he filled in. 'So why *are* you a lawyer instead of an artist?'

'Because I'm a coward,' she said, and kissed him.

When she broke the kiss, he stroked her face. 'Nice line in distraction techniques, Ms Sheridan. I get the message. But the point of this week is talking things through with someone who isn't going to sit in judgement and might give you a different perspective on the situation.'

'I don't know you well enough to talk, just yet,' she admitted.

'Then get to know me over the next few days,' he suggested. 'All you have to do is say one little word. Three letters. Starting with a Y, ending with an S, and an E in the middle.' He moved one hand to cup her breast, teasing her nipple with his forefinger and thumb. 'Your body's saying it, Lydia,' he added huskily.

'My body's an entirely different three-letter word,' she said dryly. 'It has an E in the middle, but it starts with an S.'

'That, too.' He loved fencing verbally with her. 'So is that a yes?'

For a moment, he thought she was going to say

it. Then she frowned. 'One other thing. This is just between you and me? Nobody's going to talk about it when we get back to London?'

He stared at her, not understanding. 'How do you mean, talk about it?'

'I don't want people saying that I'm trying to sleep my way to a promotion.'

'They can't, because there isn't a vacancy for you to be promoted to.' He kissed the tip of her nose. 'Stop worrying. You're on holiday. So am I. Nobody's going to ask questions.'

'I suppose not.'

'So what's the verdict?'

'I…' She blew out a breath. 'OK. I'll be brave. It's a yes.'

She muttered something else against his shoulder, clearly not intending him to catch it—but there was nothing wrong with his hearing. His ears, unlike other parts of his body, worked just fine. 'I'm not going to be disappointed.'

Her face went crimson. 'Remind me that you have bat ears, too.'

'Stop worrying.' He kissed the curve of her neck. 'This is a week out of time. Just you and me and nothing in between.' He paused. 'Is there anywhere or anything in Norway you'd particularly like to see?'

'Just the Northern Lights.'

'Then we'll go north, and hopefully we'll be lucky with the weather. I have a few places in mind, too.'

'Such as?'

'Half the fun for me will be seeing your face and watching your reaction. So I'm not going to tell you,' he said. 'Trust me. It's going to be fun.'

'Good.' Her stomach rumbled, and she flushed. 'Sorry.'

'My fault. I took you to bed instead of feeding you.' He glanced at his watch. 'It's late. We could go out, if you like. Or we could order room service…and have a bath while we're waiting.'

'A bath?' Her eyes widened.

Clearly she'd never shared a bath with a lover before. Good. He was going to enjoy this week—sharing new experiences with her. 'I have bubbles,' he tempted. 'Lots of bubbles.'

'Then how about we have a smorgasbord or something?'

'That's Swedish. Here, it's called a *koltbord*.' He gave her a sidelong look. 'So you owe me a forfeit, Ms Sheridan, for trying to be smart and getting it wrong.'

'A forfeit, hmm?' To his delight, instead of backing away, she clearly realised that he was playing and her eyes sparkled with sudden mischief. 'And what might that be?'

He loved this new, playful side of her. And he hoped he'd be able to tempt her into showing him more of it. 'I'll think about it while you run us a bath—and while I'm ordering dinner.'

'Yes, sir.' She gave him a mocking salute, then

wriggled to the edge of the bed. 'Um. Would you mind handing me some of my clothes? Or can I borrow your shirt?'

She'd gone shy on him again. He retrieved his shirt from the floor and handed it to her. 'Are you telling me we're going to have a bath together with you wearing that…oh, hang on.' He gave her a broad smile. 'You, in nothing but a shirt. White cotton, which goes see-through when it's wet. Yep. That works for me.'

'Behave.' But she was smiling as she walked to the bathroom.

Lydia had just finished running the bath when Jake walked in. 'Hi.'

'Hi.' Crazy how her heart seemed to turn over when he smiled at her.

'Lots of bubbles. Good.'

But she could see the set of his shoulders. He was tense: and she had no idea why. Was he worried that she was going to change her mind about this? Or had he changed his mind about this week with her and wasn't sure what to say to let her down gently?

'Is everything OK?' she asked diffidently.

'It's a little bright in here. Too bad we don't have any candles.'

'You've done this a lot, then.' Which meant he had high standards. Ones she would have trouble meeting.

As if he guessed at the cause of her own sudden

tension, he stroked her face. 'Not that often, no. Do you mind if I open the door and turn the overhead light off in here? That way it won't be completely dark, but it isn't eye-wateringly bright and we can just relax.'

'Sure. I, um, hope the temperature of the water's OK. I ran it the way I like it.'

He tested it with his hand. 'It's fine, Lydia,' he said with a smile. And then he looked at her. 'You look worried. Am I that scary?'

'No.' She frowned. 'And I'm not worried.' Well, only a little bit. This was on the edge of her comfort zone.

'Unconfident, then.'

'I'm not unconfident, either.'

'You are about your job. You underestimate yourself.'

She shook her head. 'I know I do a good job. I make sure I do. I just…don't want to be a lawyer any more.'

'You want to be an artist.'

'Which doesn't mean I think I'm a bad lawyer.'

'OK. I misread you wanting to change your career as a confidence wobble.' He tipped his head slightly on one side. 'But what about your sketching? You wouldn't show anyone your sketches at the Pedersens'. So you're not confident about that?'

'I sketched the children right in front of them— and I was happy to give them the sketches.'

'But you still kept a tight hand on your sketchbook.'

'That's because…' She blew out a breath. 'I *know* I can draw, Jake. My first memory is of picking up a pencil and drawing. For me, it's like breathing.'

'So why be shy about your sketchbook?'

'Because of the subject matter.'

'I don't get it. You were drawing clouds on the aeroplane.'

She flushed, and he raised an eyebrow. 'And then you turned delightfully pink. Just as you have now.'

'Because I wasn't just sketching clouds. I was drawing a picture in my head.'

He tipped his head to one side. 'What were you drawing?'

She sighed. 'I'll show you later.'

'Tell me now.'

She folded her arms. 'I was sketching *you*, all right?'

He blinked. 'Me?'

'You have a gorgeous bone structure. And your colouring…every time I saw you in the office, I wanted to paint you.'

He looked stunned. 'I've never thought of myself as an artist's model.'

'Well, now you know.' And because he'd pushed her, she lifted her chin and pushed right back. 'Actually, this week, there is something I want to do. I want to paint you.' Her eyes met his in challenge. 'Naked.'

He kissed the corner of her mouth. 'I'm terribly

flattered. But posing naked… I don't think so. No matter how good you are at art.'

'Chicken?' She scooped a handful of bubbles from the surface of the water and dabbed them on his nose. 'It's not as if I'm asking to exhibit a nude painting of you in the middle of a London gallery.'

'You're not going to exhibit a nude painting of me *anywhere*.' Mischief lit his gaze. 'Besides, you already owe me a forfeit.'

That flicker of amusement in his face—she knew he was laughing with her, not at her—gave her courage. She took his shirt off, folded her arms under her breasts, and gave him her best attempt at a sexy pout. 'How's this?'

'Not quite what I had in mind, but thank you for the view. I like it.' He picked her up and lowered her into the bath.

He looked almost as if he were about to say something; then clearly he changed his mind, because he opened the bathroom door and turned off the overhead light.

And then he stripped off.

She couldn't really see him properly in the dim light, but the outline was enough to confirm what she'd already thought. 'Wow. I stand by what I said. You're a beautiful man, Jakob Andersen. And I would really, really like to paint you.'

'As I said, I'm no model. And I'm getting cold out here. Move up.' He climbed in behind her, drawing her close so that her head rested against his chest and his hands splayed over her ribcage. There was no need for words: the moment was simply perfect.

Eventually, they heard a knock on the door.

'I'll get it,' Jake said, and dropped a kiss on the curve of her neck. 'Stay put.' He hauled himself out of the bath and wrapped a towel round himself before padding to the door to his suite.

He returned bearing a single glass and a bottle of champagne.

Champagne that would've been far from cheap in London and she knew would be eye-wateringly expensive in Norway.

'Jake, I'm…'

He pressed the tip of his forefinger lightly against her lips. 'Humour me. I thought we'd have bubbles with our bubbles. Dinner's cold so it doesn't matter when we eat.' He poured champagne into the glass, stood the glass and bottle on the edge of the bath, then untucked his towel and climbed back into the bath with her.

'This is utterly decadent,' she said when he'd fed her a sip of champagne.

'But not quite perfect. We need candlelight,' he said. 'Next time we share a bath, it'll be candlelit.'

'I'll hold you to that.' She twisted to press a kiss against his chest.

When the water grew cooler and they'd finished their second shared glass of champagne, Jake said softly, 'Time to move, *min kjære*, before we turn into prunes.' He climbed out of the bath and wrapped a towel round himself before lifting her out, drying her, and wrapping her in a soft fluffy white robe. Then he took her by the hand and led her back into the sitting room they'd used earlier as an office. To Lydia's pleasure, there was a feast laid out on the table: *gravet laks*, a selection of cheeses and salads, sliced meats and rye bread, crayfish, and something she didn't recognise.

'What's this?' she asked, gesturing to the small brown square.

'*Gjetost*. It's cheese. But maybe not quite what you would expect from cheese.' He smiled. 'Leave it until last.'

Lydia thoroughly enjoyed sitting on the sofa with him, sampling all the delicacies while they looked out over Oslo, the city's lights reflecting like stars in the fjord.

And she found out exactly why Jake had told her to leave the cheese until last when he cut her a wafer-thin slice and slid it between her lips. 'It tastes of caramel. It's wonderful.'

'It's a Norwegian speciality. I used to love it, as a child.'

She glanced at the table. 'What, no cake?' she teased.

'No. But we'll have waffles and hot chocolate for breakfast.' He kissed her lightly, then glanced at the champagne bottle. 'I think—you, me, bed. Unless you'd rather go back to your own room?'

'It'd be a bit difficult to have a hot affair in two separate rooms,' she pointed out.

'Unless we have phone sex,' he said thoughtfully. 'I could make all sorts of improper suggestions to you.'

She laughed. 'I think I'd rather have the real thing. And besides, I owe you a forfeit. I'm planning to blow your mind, the way you blew mine.'

Jake's eyes glittered. 'Tell me more.'

'Better than that,' she said, fortified by the look of sheer desire on his face. She picked up the champagne bottle. 'I'll show you.' And she sauntered back towards his bedroom, beckoning him to follow.

CHAPTER FIVE

'LYDIA. Time to get up, *min kjære*.' Jake punctuated the words with a trail of soft kisses along her shoulder.

Lydia stirred and rolled onto her back. 'What time is it?'

'Half-past seven.'

Jake hadn't bothered drawing the curtains, the previous night. 'It's still dark outside.'

'Yes, but it's not raining,' he said, 'so we're going to be lucky with the sunrise.' He nuzzled her collarbone. 'Come on. Time for a shower.'

'You're showering with me?'

For a moment he tensed. Then he smiled. 'Sounds good to me.'

Strange how such a beautiful man could still be shy with her—especially as they'd spent the entire night naked in each other's arms. But he'd been careful to keep the lights low. Was he worried that she'd assess him mentally and draw him naked without his permission, then exhibit the painting? Of course she wouldn't do that. And although she wanted to reassure him, it wasn't exactly the easiest of subjects to bring up. Maybe he'd relax with her later in the day, as she was beginning to relax with him, and they could talk about it then.

She let him lead her to the bathroom; the shower cubicle was large enough for them to shower together, and she thoroughly enjoyed soaping his chest and watching his eyes darken with arousal.

But when her hands started to drift lower, he stopped her. 'You,' he said, kissing her, 'are utterly gorgeous, and I'm very tempted to lift you up against that wall right now—but I don't want you to miss the sunrise. So we're putting this on hold.' His gaze held her. 'For now.' He brushed his mouth against hers, then turned off the water and wrapped her in a towel. 'How long is it going to take you to get dressed?'

'In what I was wearing last night?'

'No.' He kissed the tip of her nose. 'I'll check the corridor for you, but I'm pretty sure you can sneak next door in a bathrobe.'

'Right.' Sneaking next door in a bathrobe. They really hadn't thought this through properly, last night.

He rubbed the pad of his thumb along her lower lip. 'You have your stern lawyer face on. Remember, we're playing hookey.'

'Uh-huh.'

He sighed. 'Give me your key, *elskling*. I'll go and fetch you something.'

'No, it's OK.' She gave a dismissive shrug. 'I'm being silly.'

'Not silly. You're thinking. And this week isn't a normal week. It's seven days stolen from real life, to have fun and talk about our dreams and sort a few things out in our heads. That's what we agreed, yes?'

'Yes.'

'Go and get dressed. But don't take too long. It's only breakfast—casual will do fine.'

'Not all women take hours to get ready, you know,' she pointed out.

'You certainly don't need make-up. You're beautiful as you are.' He smiled. 'And I have to admit, I like you slightly ruffled.' He leaned forward so he could whisper in her ear, and his breath was warm against her skin. 'It makes you look sexy as hell.'

She was more used to criticism than praise but, instead of making her feel uncomfortable and embarrassed, his words made her feel as if she were walking on air. The fact that an amazing man like Jake Andersen could feel that way about her made her blood sing.

Well, hey. Not every man was like Robbie. It was more than time that she got over that. 'Give me five minutes,' she said, exchanging her towel for the robe and wrapping a hand towel round her wet hair.

And in precisely five minutes he knocked on her door.

It was the first time she'd ever seen him in jeans:

soft, slightly faded denim, teamed with a black polo-necked cashmere sweater. In a formal business suit, Jake was good-looking but had a faintly remote air. In casual clothes, he looked like a Viking pirate. Particularly as he hadn't stopped to shave. Dangerous, sexy as hell, and her knees turned to water.

'Come and have breakfast,' he said, taking her hand and drawing her into the hallway. 'Got your key?'

She nodded.

'And your camera? Because, trust me, you're going to want to photograph this.'

'Two seconds.' She went back into her room, grabbed her camera from her bedside drawer and closed the door behind her. As they walked down the corridor he laced his fingers through hers.

In the restaurant, he chose them a table by the window, overlooking the city to the east. 'Can I tempt you to my favourite breakfast?'

He could tempt her, full stop, she thought. 'Sure.'

A few minutes later, the waitress brought them mugs of hot chocolate and a pile of waffles.

'Heart-shaped. That's very…' she smiled '…romantic.'

'It's the proper shape for Norwegian *vafler*. The waffle iron looks like a flower—they're made in fours.' He placed a couple of hearts on a plate, then added what looked like apricot jam and yoghurt; he passed the plate over to her, and helped himself to the same.

'Jam and yoghurt?' she asked.

'Compote and sour cream,' he corrected, and took a mouthful of his own breakfast. 'Mmm. Not quite up to *Farmor*'s recipe—my Norwegian grandmother's,' he said. 'But close.'

She tried it. The waffle was good, soft and fluffy, but she didn't recognise the taste of the amber-coloured jam. It was tart and sweet at the same time, and she loved it. 'What kind of compote is it?'

'Cloudberry. Obviously it's the wrong time of year for fresh ones, but when they're in season, they're something else. They look like pale gold blackberries. And they taste,' he said, 'like heaven.'

She believed him. But when the cloudberries were next in season—presumably the summer— she and Jake would be in very different places. Definitely not together.

She pushed the thought away. They were supposed to be living in the present, for this week. No regrets, no recriminations.

It was still early enough for them to be the only ones in the restaurant; when they'd finished their waffles, Jake came round to her side of the table, manoeuvred her out of her chair, then sat her on his lap. 'Watch,' he said.

A thin ribbon of yellow appeared on the horizon; as the sun began to rise, the sky began to be streaked with pink and yellow and lilac. Lit by the sun, the clouds looked as if they were lined with pure gold. And the whole thing was reflected in the fjord. Lydia had never seen such a breath-taking sunrise: even her favourite part of Italy wasn't this exotic at sunrise, like an orchid unfold-ing across the sky

'You're right. I need to photograph this,' she said, awed. And later, she'd draw it in pastels. She took shot after shot until the sun had risen completely.

'I can't believe the colours,' she said, leaning back against him. 'That was stunning. Thank you.'

'If we're lucky, we might get to see mother-of-pearl clouds some time this week.'

'Mother-of-pearl clouds?'

'Nacreous clouds. You sometimes see them just before dawn or just after sunset.' He took his mobile phone from his pocket and flicked into the internet. A few moments later, he'd found a picture for her. 'Like this.'

She could see where the name came from. The clouds had the same sheen and shimmer as mother-of-pearl. 'I like that. It makes me want to paint it.'

He flicked onto another page and showed her a picture of an arc of light; it looked a bit like a rainbow, but it had what looked like a martini glass made from rainbows shimmering in the centre.

'Very clever photography,' she said.

'No, it's the real thing—it's an ice halo and a sun pillar. You see it when the sun's low and reflects on the ice crystals in the sky. I've only seen it once, in Norway—I was a child, and I thought it was as if a spider had spun a web of rainbows across the whole sky.'

'That's beautiful.'

He wrapped his arms round her and kissed the sensitive spot behind her ear. 'I need maybe half an hour to make some calls. I'll book a flight up north and sort out hotel reservations. Then we'll go shopping, and I'll show you round the city.'

'Fine by me. Just knock on my door when you're ready to go.'

They walked back to their rooms together, and Lydia transferred the photographs to her laptop; she chose her favourite one, then grabbed her pastels and the spiral-bound pad of pastel paper and began copying the lines of the sunrise, smudging the colours together with the side of her little finger. She grew so involved in what she was doing that she completely lost track of time and started when she heard the knock on the door.

'Ready?' Jake asked when she answered.

'I just need to clean my hands.'

'May I?' he asked, glancing over to her open pad.

'Be my guest.'

He was looking through the pad when she came out of the bathroom. 'I'm impressed.'

'Thank you.'

'And I feel almost guilty about dragging you

away from sketching—but we're going north. Which means we need clothes.'

'I already have clothes. You told me to bring layers.' She gestured to the long-sleeved T-shirt she wore under a V-necked sweater.

He shook his head. 'Not enough. And jeans are fine for here, but not for further north. Gloves?'

She took them from her coat pocket.

He grimaced. 'You'll freeze. They're not heavy duty enough for where we're going. You'll need another pair on top. Swimming costume?'

She blinked. 'If it's cold enough for me to need extra gloves, why on earth would I want a swimming costume?'

'For the hot tub—well, unless we had a very private one,' he said with a grin. 'In which case you'd need nothing at all, *elskling*.'

Oh, the picture that put in her head.

'Right. Let's hit the shops.'

Because the hotel was central, they were soon in Karl Johans Gate, the main shopping street of the city. Lydia was entranced by the beautiful four-storey buildings, their upper storeys painted colours of ice cream and the windows painted white.

'It's really pretty in summer—they have little awnings over the windows, like the hoods of old-fashioned prams,' Jake told her.

She could well imagine it.

'The royal castle's at the other end of the street,'

he said. 'Once we've got the clothes sorted, we'll do the touristy stuff.' He took her into one of the department stores. He walked swiftly through the women's department, picking out fleece-lined trousers and a variety of cashmere and fleecy tops. 'You'll need to layer them, and wool's much better than cotton,' he said. 'Go and try them on.'

They were the perfect fit. But when she came out of the changing rooms to discover that Jake had picked up some thermal underwear and thick socks, as well as a very demure swimming costume, she burst out laughing.

'What?'

'We're supposed to be having a hot affair. And you're making me buy the unsexiest underwear in the world.'

He moved closer, and whispered in her ear, 'Firstly, *I'm* buying. No arguments. Secondly, where I'm planning to take you, you'll definitely need thermals. And, thirdly, I guarantee I can make them sexy.'

She could feel his breath against her skin, and it made her shiver in anticipation. 'That's a guarantee, is it?' To her disgust, her voice was slightly shaky.

'It's a promise. And I always keep my promises.'

She didn't trust herself to speak, after that. Didn't say a word when Jake picked up an armful of clothes for himself—which he didn't bother trying on— and a suitcase. And she made no protest when Jake took out his credit card at the cash desk. He'd made it clear that he wanted to do this. And she could always insist on treating him to dinner and maybe buy him something later, to keep things equal.

He arranged to have the shopping delivered to the hotel, then turned to her again. 'Do you have any sunglasses with you?'

'No.'

'You'll need them.'

She frowned. 'Why? I thought the north was meant to have polar nights, so it's practically twilight?'

'You'll still get reflections from the snow. You need glasses. And a hat. As do I.' He led her through to a display of hats, and donned a deerstalker with flappy bits over the ears. She burst out laughing.

'Laugh all you like, *min kjære*,' he said loftily. 'But when your ears hurt with the cold and mine are toasty-warm…'

But he put the hat back, smiling at her. And then he picked up a Russian hat. 'Before you ask, it's not real fur. It's synthetic and it's lined with fleece,' he said, correctly interpreting the look in her face.

He put the hat on.

She raised an eyebrow. 'You look like a rock star.'

'Not quite.' He took dark glasses from his inside coat pocket and slid them on. 'How about now?'

She laughed. 'You'll do. And, by the way, I'm buying the hats.'

'You don't need to.'

'But I want to.' She threw his words back at him. 'No arguments.'

'All right. Then thank you.' He nuzzled her ear lobe and whispered, 'I'll thank you properly later.'

Desire rippled all the way down her spine as she imagined just how he'd thank her.

Pulling herself together, she chose a hat like his, but grey rather than black. 'Do I look completely ridiculous in this?' she asked, trying it on.

'You look gorgeous.' He lowered his voice. 'And I'm expecting you to pose for me in it, later. You, high heels and that hat.'

She could just imagine it, and it made lust shimmer all the way through her. And the appreciation in his gaze was enough to give her the confidence to riposte, 'Only if you do the same.'

He laughed. 'I don't suit high heels, *elskling*.'

She couldn't help laughing back. 'You're impossible, Jakob Andersen.'

'Now we're playing tourist,' he said, and tucked her arm through his. She felt like a million dollars, walking by his side; and she was glad of the hat and glasses. Even though it was a winter sun, it was still bright; and the lack of cloud cover meant that the temperature had dropped.

He clearly knew the city well, showing her the sights—the royal castle, the Oslo *rådhus*—and then he took her into the Viking ship museum to see the preserved ships.

She studied a narrow boat with its curved prow and serpentine coil. 'I can just see you standing in the boat, ordering your men to row faster.'

'I'd ask, not order,' he corrected. Then he smiled. 'But you're nearer the mark than you think. I grew up in boats. Every summer, I'd come to Norway and explore the fjords with my grandfather. We'd go fishing, but I loved exploring. And sometimes I pretended to be a Viking warrior, coming to find new lands.'

'New people to conquer?'

'Trade with,' he said, 'rather than conquer. And *Farfar*—my grandfather—taught me about iolite.'

'Iolite?' She searched her memory. 'Isn't that a blue stone? Used in jewellery?'

'It is, now. But the Vikings used it as a polarising filter—they also used to call it the sunstone. They'd cut a thin slice, so they could look through it and see the exact position of the sun to help them navigate.'

There was a paperweight made from a cube of iolite in the gift shop, and Jake bought it. 'As an artist, I think you'll appreciate this,' he said, handing her the bag.

'Thank you. It's a beautiful colour.'

'Take it out and play with it,' he said.

She did so and discovered that the violet-blue cube looked clear as water from one side, and honey-yellow at the top. 'It's an optical thing, isn't it? It's how prisms work, too, by refracting light.'

He nodded. 'It's also known as the water sapphire, because of the way the colour changes.'

'Sunstone, water sapphire… It's beautiful,' she said appreciatively. She bought postcards of the ships and a book. 'Emma will just love showing these to the kids.'

'Your best friend has children?'

'She teaches Year Three—eight-year-olds. I think they're doing a topic on the Vikings in the summer term,' Lydia explained.

'Uh-huh.'

With that set look on his face, she knew that Jake had gone remote on her again. There was definitely a problem where children were concerned. Part of her wanted to encourage him to talk about it—after all, they'd agreed that this was a week of bouncing ideas off each other—but she had a feeling that this was something that went really deep. Something he needed a little more time to open up about. So instead, she said softly, 'Come and show me more of Oslo. Nils and Elisabet said I'd like the opera house.'

'You will.'

They were right. She couldn't take her eyes off the angular building with its glass and white stone reflected in the water below, and she loved the idea that she could walk on the top. 'This is stunning, Jake. I can see why you love Norway so much. The architecture, the scenery, the people…' She smiled at him. 'Thank you for this.'

'Pleasure,' he said, giving her a tiny bow.

And then he took her to the Munch museum. 'I can't not take an artist to see Norway's most famous painting, can I?' he asked dryly as they stood in front of 'The Scream'.

Wandering through the art gallery hand in hand with Jake was something else. The etching of Munch's 'The Kiss' made her want to slide her arms round Jake's neck and pull his head down to hers, just like the models for the etching.

But then he took her to the other prized possession in the museum: 'Madonna'.

And it was utterly stunning.

'Jake, that's beautiful. The colours—the sheer sensuality.' Her fingers tightened round his.

'It makes you want to reach out and touch her, doesn't it?' he asked.

'If I were a man, maybe it would,' she said with a smile. 'But what it makes me want to do is paint a certain person naked from the waist upwards, lying on a bed and looking completely abandoned to pleasure.'

'Naked from the waist upwards,' he repeated thoughtfully. 'So your model could drape a sheet round his hips.'

She raised an eyebrow. 'I'd make the painting modest. But this particular model…I want him completely naked. Comfortable in his own skin. And thinking about just what I'm offering him to pose for me.'

'Which is?'

Feeling bold, she reached up on tiptoe and whispered in his ear.

Jake sucked in a breath. 'Lydia, we can't have this conversation in a public place.'

He was tempted. She could see it in his face. 'So what do you suggest?'

'I'll finish playing tourist with you, while it's still light. And then we'll have this conversation somewhere a little more private.'

He took her to the Frogner district, where they wandered through streets with tiny antique shops nestling beside modern designer shops. Lydia spotted a pair of earrings in a window. 'Do you mind if I go in and buy these?'

He looked surprised. 'Your ears aren't pierced.'

'Polly's are—my godmother,' she explained. 'And this is perfect for her for Christmas. The design's really unusual so she'll love them.'

'The design?' he asked.

'She notices that sort of thing because she's a designer. Dresses.' She smiled wryly. 'I still have no idea how she's my mother's best friend. I know they met as students—but they're practically complete opposites.'

'You're close to Polly?'

She nodded. 'I can talk to her.'

'And she's a designer,' he said. 'So she knows how you feel about your art?'

'Yes.' She sighed. 'My parents think I gave up all that nonsense before university. I don't talk about it to them. But Polly's always encouraged me.'

'I'm glad,' he said, 'that you have someone on your side. It's what you really want to do, isn't it?'

'I've been fighting it for a long, long time,' she admitted. 'I think maybe it's time to give in. To follow my heart instead of my head.'

'Are they necessarily two different things?'

She spread her hands. 'I don't know. Maybe.'

'So what's holding you back? Money?'

'No. I know my earnings won't be anywhere near what my salary is now, until I'm really well established, but I have enough savings to keep me going for a while.'

'Then what's stopping you?'

'I don't know.'

'Yes, you do,' he said softly. 'Say it out loud. Because that makes the barrier smaller.'

Trust him to cut to the chase. But maybe he had a point. She took a deep breath. 'Habit. I suppose. And maybe a bit of fear, too. I know I can draw, but so can plenty of other people. Am I really outstanding enough to make it work?'

'Sometimes,' he said, 'you have to take a risk. A calculated one. And you do have a fallback position. You can always go back to law if it doesn't work out. Or if you don't want to take such a big step, you could try doing both part time.'

'I thought about working part time as an artist,' she said. 'But then I wouldn't be giving it my best shot. I'd only be putting half my energy into it. And if it's worth doing, it's worth doing with a whole heart. Your Vikings didn't say they'd spend three days a week exploring and three days a week fishing in the river at home, did they?'

'True.' He squeezed her hand. 'It sounds to me as if you've made your decision.'

'What about you?' she asked.

'Me? I'm fine.'

She didn't believe a word of it, but she hadn't worked out the right questions to ask—questions that would persuade him to talk instead of putting up that invisible and impenetrable wall. 'In that case, let's go and get Polly's earrings.'

She bought a second pair, too.

'For your best friend?' he guessed.

She nodded. 'Emma loves silver. And this glass is gorgeous. It could almost tempt me into doing a still life.'

'You're not wearing any jewellery,' he noted.

'Only my watch,' she said. 'But I could be very tempted by these.' She gestured towards the display of bracelets with silver and glass beads threaded onto them as they left the shop. 'I love the colours of the glass. Especially the blue ones.'

'Your favourite colour?' he guessed.

She nodded. 'Sapphire blue.' The same colour

as Jake's eyes. Intense. The colour of a sunlit Norwegian sky.

'Then you'll like the blue hour.'

'The blue hour?' she repeated, mystified.

'The last hour before sunset, when the light seems almost blue. It's a shame it isn't snowing, because the park's really something in the snow.'

'The park' turned out to be Vigeland Park, full of sculptures in granite, bronze and cast iron. Lydia loved every second of it, and she was stunned by the fourteen-metre-high monolith in the centre.

'However long must it have taken to carve that?' she marvelled.

'Actually, that's a known fact. Vigeland modelled it in clay, then had this huge block of granite brought to the park. It took a team of three stone carvers fourteen years to transfer the figures to the granite.'

'It's stunning—and I love the way people are holding each other so tightly. It's hope, isn't it?'

'That's one interpretation, yes.'

She tightened her arm round his waist. 'Jake, you've given me such a perfect day. Taken me to see such wonderful things. The ships, that incredible painting and now this.'

'My pleasure. And you've given me something back—you've made me see it all afresh through your eyes. That sense of wonder.'

'Go and stand against the monolith,' she said, 'so I can take a picture.'

She did so, zooming in on the figures and then, on impulse, zooming in on Jake's face.

'Would you like me to take your photograph together?' a soft voice asked.

She looked over at Jake for confirmation; when he gave the tiniest nod, she smiled at the tourist who'd spoken to her. 'Yes, please. That's very kind of you. *Takk.*'

Jake held her close in front of him, wrapping his arms round her waist and pressing his cheek against hers. As they smiled for the camera she realised just how easy it would be to fall in love with him.

But that wasn't the deal.

And she needed to remember that.

This was a week out of time. For both of them. And after that…she had no idea what the future would hold.

CHAPTER SIX

ON THE way back from the park, Jake found a small café. 'Let's have dinner here.'

Lydia loved the atmosphere as soon as she walked in. Sturdy wooden tables, low lights, and a woman playing the piano and singing jazz songs. Perfect.

Except for the fact that the menu was written entirely in Norwegian.

'I could translate for you,' Jake said. 'Or you can trust me to order for us both.'

Trust.

She'd relied entirely on herself for the last ten years.

But this was a week out of time. And trust wasn't an issue, where Jake was concerned. She'd spent the night with him, told him her dreams. 'Order for me,' she said.

'Is there any food in particular you don't like?'

'Offal—oh, and Brussels sprouts.'

He smiled. 'Noted. And do you like red wine?'

'Yes, but one glass will be enough for me, so don't feel you need to order a whole bottle.' She wanted to keep her head clear enough to persuade Jake to pose for her, and then to sketch him in pastels, the way she'd seen him in her mind's eye.

'One glass will do me, too. I'll be back in a minute.' He went to the bar to order for them, and her fingers itched to capture the scene. The way he leaned against the wooden counter, one foot resting casually on the brass bar at the base, made the curve of his bottom look absolutely perfect.

He returned to their table with two glasses of red wine just as she was about to put her sketchbook back in her handbag.

'Show me.' It was an invitation rather than an order.

She handed the book across without comment.

He raised an eyebrow at the last sketch in the book. 'Sneaky.'

'Irresistible,' she countered. 'You know what you were saying about that painting making you want to touch?'

'Mmm-hmm.'

'Well, *that*,' she said huskily, 'is what makes me want to touch. And I have every intention of doing so, later.'

He moistened his lower lip. 'I'm very tempted to tell them to cancel our order and take you straight back to the hotel.'

'No.' She reached out and entwined her fingers with his. 'I like this place. And I like sharing this with you. Spending time with you.'

'Me, too,' he said, leaving his hand exactly where it was while he leafed through the sketchpad with his free hand. 'These are seriously good, Lydia,' he said when he'd finished. 'And I'm not flattering you. I'm not artistic myself, but I can appreciate other people's work. I know when a boat design will work, because I can see the final thing in my mind's eye from the blueprint. And these make me see in three-D, too.'

'So are you going to let me do a proper portrait? Not just sneak it in when you're looking the other way?'

He looked thoughtful. 'And your audience would be…?'

Strange that a man who was so confident in business was so shy about his appearance. Especially because he was one of the most beautiful men she'd ever seen. Women must've thrown themselves at him in droves; he had to know how gorgeous he was.

No, there was a reason for this odd shyness. She just hadn't worked out what it was, yet. But right now she needed to reassure him that he wasn't taking a stupid risk. 'It'll be for my eyes only. That's a promise.' She paused. 'And I keep my promises, Jake.'

'I'll think about it. But I'm not making any promises, OK?'

'OK.'

The meal, when it arrived, was beautifully presented: rack of lamb with a rich red sauce, simple boiled potatoes and steamed green vegetables, on a deep blue plate. She tasted the sauce. 'It's gorgeous. Red wine and…what, redcurrant?'

'Lingonberry,' he said. 'We don't get them so much in England, so I suppose the nearest equivalent is cranberry.'

'It's lovely. If I could cook, I'd be tempted to make this.'

'You can't cook?' He looked surprised.

She wrinkled her nose. 'I can do the basics. But cooking isn't really my thing.'

'You'd rather spend your time painting.'

'Yes.'

'So I guess you'd need a life partner who can cook.'

'Not everyone wants a life partner,' she said, thinking about Robbie and how he'd dumped her at the first major hurdle their relationship had faced. She hoped she had steered Jake away from the subject.

'So you're saying you don't want a partner and children? A family?' He raised an eyebrow. 'And yet you're good with kids. You were so patient with Morten and Kristin.'

'I like children,' she said. She ate a few more mouthfuls, but he didn't change the conversation; he simply waited for her to expand her answer. Clearly he wasn't going to let her off the hook. She sighed. 'All right. Yes. In an ideal world, I'd like a family of my own, at some time in the future.' The thought filled her with a bittersweet pain. Lydia knew the family she dreamed of would not be the kind of family she had grown up with. If she ever found the perfect person to have children with she would not make the same mistakes her parents had made. She'd encourage her children to go for their dreams and above all else be happy.

Jake wished he hadn't pushed her, now. The snippets Lydia had told him about her parents had made him realise that her childhood had been very different from his: she obviously hadn't had the loving and supportive parents he'd been privileged to have. And he'd thought—hoped, maybe—that because of her upbringing, she might not want children. And that would make the possibility of a relationship between them just that bit more likely.

How foolish he'd been.

'But you don't, do you?'

He really hadn't expected the question, and he felt his eyes widen. 'What makes you say that?'

'Because every time either of us has mentioned children, you've gone really quiet.' She reached across the table and tangled her fingers in his. 'Given that you're close to your family, I'm guessing there's another reason for it. Someone's hurt you, too.'

She was right on the money, there. Maybe it was the artist in her, but it was as if she could see right through him—right through the charming, urbane exterior that kept everyone else at bay.

Tonight, if he let her paint him, she'd see the rest. Because she'd want enough light to see him properly. She'd see and she'd ask questions. Panic flared through him. He couldn't do this.

Her fingers tightened round his. 'What was it you told me? Say it out loud, because it makes things smaller. You were right. It works.'

Maybe. But no amount of talking would make his problem smaller. It wasn't fixable. Just…in abeyance.

For now.

'Jake?' she prompted softly.

He could tell her some of it. Just not all of it.

'I was engaged. But it didn't work out.'

'She wasn't the one?'

'No.' Though at one point he'd thought she was. Grace by name, graceful by nature. Sweet and pretty and delicate.

Too delicate, as it turned out.

'Don't feel sorry for me,' he added. 'I was the one who broke it off.' It was true—up to a point. Grace had wanted to end it, but she'd been trapped. What kind of woman walked out on the man she was supposed to love, at the first hint of things being sticky? What would people think about her? He'd seen it all in her eyes. The panic and the guilt.

And the pity.

That had been the hardest part. Facing her pity. Something he never, ever wanted to see again in anyone's eyes.

'We wanted different things,' he added, to stave off her next question.

That wasn't strictly true. He'd wanted exactly what Grace wanted; he just hadn't been able to give it to her. So he'd known he had to let her go. If he'd asked her to stay, she would've ended up resenting him for it, maybe even hating him.

He'd known he'd done the right thing when he'd seen the relief in Grace's eyes. The relief of knowing that she had the chance of a normal life and a normal family, without having to go through the mill of IVF or the intrusive questions before formal adoption. The relief of knowing she wasn't likely to be left a widow when the children were still very young, and have to cope on her own.

'So she wanted children?' Lydia asked softly.

'Yes. And I don't think it's fair to have kids if you're concentrating on your career. You need to make time for a family.' All true: he believed every single word he was saying. But it was also all a smokescreen, and he hoped she'd draw the conclusion that he wanted to concentrate on his career instead of guessing the truth he was trying to hide. That he wanted a family more than anything else on earth, but he'd made the decision not to be selfish about it because his future held no guarantees and it just wasn't fair to dump that kind of burden on someone.

But then Lydia flinched, and he realised that he'd just trampled over one of her own sore spots. Her parents hadn't supported her dreams, so it was a fair bet that they'd also concentrated on their careers and hadn't had time for her.

'Maybe,' he said carefully, 'we should change the subject. I don't think this is a comfortable one for either of us.'

'No. Which gives us the option of facing it, or being chicken and avoiding it.'

'There's a third option,' he said. 'Moving out of our comfort zones a little bit at a time.'

'Half a chicken,' she mused.

'Works for me.'

They ate in silence for the rest of their meal, neither of them willing to risk another subject that might trample on a sore spot.

Eventually, he sighed. 'Lydia.'

'Yes?'

'You're tense. So am I. And there's only one cure I know that really works. Give me two minutes to settle the bill.'

'No. I'm paying, tonight.'

He was about to protest when she added softly, 'This week, we're equals, remember.'

So she was just as proud as he was. He acknowledged it with a formal nod. 'Then thank you for dinner, *min kjære.*'

'*Vær så god.*'

You're welcome. Her pronunciation wasn't quite right, but he loved the fact that she'd tried.

Funny, when he'd brought Grace to Norway, she hadn't tried to learn a single thing. At the time, he'd enjoyed the fact that she thought he was so reliable and she'd leaned on him. Now he recognised the puffed-up vanity for what it was. And he knew he didn't want someone to protect, any more. He wanted someone who'd be his equal—someone who'd trust him enough to lean on him, but who would also be there for him on the rare occasions when he needed someone to lean on.

Someone like Lydia Sheridan.

He pushed the thought away. They were both at a crossroads. She needed to find her own way: which might not necessarily be the same path that he wanted. He'd take this week as they'd agreed. At face value. Someone to bounce ideas off, have fun with—and hot sex.

Nothing deeper.

And absolutely no involvement from his heart.

Once Lydia had settled the bill, Jake draped one arm round her shoulders, drawing her close; she slid her arm round his waist and tucked her hand into his. Although they walked back to the hotel in silence, it wasn't the same kind of tension as there had been in the restaurant.

This was more like anticipation.

And he really needed to lose himself in her. Just for a moment. Forget who he was.

'My room, tonight,' she said softly.

Jake wasn't arguing. But the second he'd closed the door behind them, he pulled her into his arms and kissed her deeply.

'Not so fast,' she said when he broke the kiss. 'There's something I want to do.'

He knew exactly what. 'I'm sorry. I don't think I can handle posing naked for you.'

She frowned. 'Jake, you're the most gorgeous man I've ever seen. And I've already promised you that I won't show this to anyone else. There won't be an exhibition to embarrass you or make things difficult in business.'

She really thought *that* was worrying him? But if he told her the truth…

He could handle that even less.

'If it makes you feel better,' she said, 'I've never asked anyone to sit for me before.'

That got his attention. 'Then why me?'

'Because you're beautiful,' she said simply. 'And because this is our week out of time. Fun.'

'Right.'

His scepticism must have shown in his voice, because she smiled. 'All right. I admit I'm the one who gets the fun of painting you, while you have to sit still and be very patient. But there's a saying about good things coming to those who wait.'

He felt his eyes narrow. 'What sort of good things?'

She spread her hands. 'That's up for negotiation. But starting with what I suggested in the gallery.'

He remembered. That sweet, serious mouth whispering incredibly sensual suggestions into his ear. Sheer desire poleaxed him. 'Uh,' was about all he could manage to say.

Keeping her gaze fixed on his, she lifted the hem of his sweater. 'I like this. It's soft. But not as soft as your skin,' she said. 'And it's a barrier. I want to see you, Jake.'

He had to make the decision. Push her away—or take a chance and let her do it.

Either way, he knew she'd end up asking questions.

But if he did this…he'd be facing one particular demon. Conquering it. And maybe then he'd be able to look people in the eye without fearing their pity.

He lifted his arms, letting her peel off the cashmere.

And he sucked in a breath as she undid the buttons on his jeans. He could feel his erection straining against his fly; he knew she'd noticed, because she gave a tiny little smile—a smile that told him just how much she was enjoying this—and stroked him through his underpants with her thumb and forefinger, tracing the edges of his penis.

How the hell she expected him to lie there and let her paint him, when every instinct told him to grab her, pull her onto the bed and bury himself deep inside her…

'Patience,' she said, her voice low and husky.

Either he'd spoken aloud, or she'd guessed his thoughts.

He really, really hoped it was the latter.

'It'll be worth the wait.' She dropped to her knees in front of him, making him quiver as she slowly drew the soft denim downwards. She dealt with his boots and his socks, and then he was standing before her only in his underpants, feeling ridiculously shy and gauche and unsure of himself. As if he were sixteen, not thirty.

'I've never posed for an artist before.'

'You're posing for *me,*' she said softly. 'This isn't going to hurt.'

Maybe not physically. But he could already feel the tension knotting the back of his neck.

She curled her fingers round his, then led him to the bed and pulled the duvet off. She arranged the pillows, stood back and squinted at it, then nodded. 'That'll do. Now, I want you to lie there with your right arm back behind your head—just rest your head on your hand.'

He did as she asked.

'Now your left hand. Slide it behind your back, into the hollow. Good, just like that. And your head—tilt it slightly to the left, and lift your chin up. Perfect. Is that an OK position for you?'

'I think so. Do you want my eyes closed?'

'No. I want them open.' She peeled off her sweater and rolled up the sleeves of her T-shirt. 'Munch's original is in oils, but that's not what I'm going to do. I like working in pastels. They're more immediate. Now, I'll work as fast as I can—but tell me if you feel the slightest bit uncomfortable, or if you need a break and want to move around a bit, OK?'

'OK.'

'One last thing. *Don't* move your hands,' she warned. Then she gave him a truly wicked smile, curved her fingers into the waistband of his underpants, and removed them before he'd quite realised what she was planning to do.

Too late to backtrack, now.

He'd just have to bluff his way through it. And hope that she didn't realise she was the first person to see him like this since his surgeon.

'You're perfect, Jake,' she whispered. 'Stunning.'

Perfect? He could've wept. He wasn't perfect. Wasn't *whole*.

She trailed her fingers over his ribs. Over his abdomen. Lower and lower and lower.

He was watching her face intently, and he knew the exact moment she saw the scar.

'Jake?'

'It's old.' True enough. Eighteen months was long enough to count as 'old', surely? 'Nothing important.'

And that was a complete lie.

He held his breath, waiting for her to challenge him.

To pity him.

'It's important enough to embarrass you. And that's why you always have the lights down low, I take it.'

Yes, that was his clever lawyer speaking. Getting right to the heart of things, as usual. He closed his eyes, unable to face her pity.

'You know,' she said softly, 'the carpet-makers in Persia used to deliberately weave an imperfection into the pattern of their rugs, because human craft isn't perfect. And yet that tiny imperfection actually highlights the perfection of the rest.'

He felt her mouth brush over his, and opened his eyes again.

'If you really don't want to do this,' she said quietly, 'then I won't push you. I can paint you from memory, later.'

'Scars and all?' He tried to keep his voice light.

This time, her kiss lingered. 'You trust my judgement, yes?'

Ha. He'd used exactly the same tactics on her. Where was she heading with this?

'Jake?' she prompted.

He sighed. 'I trust your judgement. As a lawyer.'

She laughed. 'Been here, done that. Let's cut through the hype.' She laid the backs of her fingers lightly against his cheek. 'My judgement's the same—lawyer or artist. I like what I see, and I want to put what I see on paper. Yes, you have scars—but they're part of you. Nobody's perfect, Jake. People have scars and birthmarks and freckles and all kinds of things they might think are imperfections, but other people don't even notice them.'

She hadn't backed away. No disgust, no pity, no guilt in her face. Concern, yes; and a bit of wariness, as if she were pushing the boundaries of her own comfort zone. And hadn't she said that she'd never asked anyone to sit for her, before? If he backed off now, he had a feeling that she'd see it as rejection of her, not his own fears getting in the way.

Besides, if he admitted that he was scared, she'd ask him why. And he'd have to tell her what lay behind his scars—something he just couldn't bring himself to do.

'Then do it,' he said, dragging in a breath. 'Do it.'

Lydia still didn't understand Jake's reluctance, but she wasn't going to argue.

'Thank you.' She kissed him swiftly on the mouth, then grabbed the box of pastels she'd put in the drawer, along with the special pad she kept for pastels. She had a box of wipes handy for cleaning her fingertips and avoiding running the wrong colours together.

She sucked in a breath. This was almost exactly what she'd seen in the gallery, in her mind's eye. There was only one thing missing from the pose: the expression of bliss on his face.

And she knew exactly how to get that.

Again, it meant moving out of her comfort zone. Taking the lead. But it was another step forward. Overcoming her barriers.

'Jake—don't move, but I want you to listen to me. When I'm done here,' she said, quickly drawing the lines of his body on the paper, 'I'm going to deliver on my promise. You'll still be lying there on a pile of pillows, but you'll have both hands behind your head. And I'm going to be kneeling beside you, naked. I'm going to kiss you—hot and wet and hungry. Open-mouthed. And then I'm going to let one hand slide down your body, stroke your skin until you're desperate for me to touch you more intimately.

'But you're not going to move your hands, Jake. Instead, you're going to let me pleasure you. And I'm going to follow my hands with my mouth. Kiss all the way down your breastbone, and you'll feel my hair drifting against your skin. Soft as a kiss. A promise of what's coming.'

Just as she'd hoped, his face changed. His mouth parted slightly; even if he hadn't been naked and fully visible to her, she would've known that he was aroused. His eyes were lit from a focus within. A focus of passion and need and desire.

She shifted slightly in her seat. It was hard to keep focused and continue sketching when she so badly wanted to touch him. When she wanted to paint his skin with the pastels, draw long, slow strokes down his body and smudge the colours with her own skin.

'I'm going to move my way slowly south, Jake. Touching and licking and kissing until you can't hold your pose any more, and your hands slide into my hair, urging me on.'

His breathing had grown deeper, now; it sounded slightly ragged as he listened to her and imagined her words becoming reality.

'And then I'm going to do what I promised. Payback. Because I'm going to take you into my mouth.'

To Lydia's intense gratification, he actually quivered.

A tiny moan of sheer need escaped him.

But he held the pose.

Jakob Andersen was a man at his peak: old enough to know, and young enough to enjoy it. Combined with that core of inner strength, it made him irresistible.

'I'm going to tease you with my lips and tongue, touch you and taste you. And you're going to see streams of light in your head as you come.'

'Uh. Lydia.' He dragged in a breath between the syllables of her name. 'You have to stop talking. Because, if you don't, I don't think I'll be able to keep myself under control for much longer.'

Mmm, and having to explain to the hotel why there was oil pigment smeared all over the crumpled white sheets wasn't something she really wanted to do.

She shut up.

Drew as fast as she could.

Radiated the colour around him.

'OK. You can move, now.'

It took him half a second to climb off the bed and yank her into his arms. His kiss was so hot, it felt as if he'd scorched her skin.

'Do you have any idea,' he said, 'how hard it was to stay put, just then?'

She wriggled slightly on his lap. 'Yeah. I can feel just how hard. *Very* nice, Mr Andersen.'

He kissed her in answer, but this time it was gentler, coaxing a response.

'Want to see?' she asked.

'Oh, yeah. I want to see. I want you naked.' He tugged at the hem of her T-shirt.

'I meant, the picture.'

'That, too.' He bared her midriff.

'Jake. My hands are covered in paint. I need to clean up.'

He took a wipe from the box and gently removed the smears of colour from her fingers. He was thorough, cleaning every centimetre of her skin, and, oddly, it made her feel cherished. Special.

She knew the second that he'd seen the picture in the open sketchpad, because he went very still.

When he hadn't said a word for two whole minutes, she said softly, 'Jake?'

'It's not often I'm speechless,' he said. 'That's… It's amazing.'

'And modest. As I promised.' She'd stopped at his waist. She pressed a kiss to his temple. 'But, as I said, this is for my personal viewing only.'

'That's how you see me?'

'It's how I saw you in my head, when we were at the gallery. And, um, how you looked when I talked to you.' And it gave her a kick to know that she'd been able to put that look of sheer desire on his face.

He drew her hand to his mouth and kissed the pulse point in her wrist. 'You're incredible. Talent like this shouldn't be locked away.'

She rested the palm of her free hand against his face, curving it round his cheek. 'I'm not the only person in the world who can draw.'

'Why are you so hard on yourself?' Jake asked.

'I'm not.' Just saying what she'd always been told. *Artists are ten a penny.*

'Or is this a creative thing? You can see the flaws because it's not as you saw things in your head, but nobody else can see inside your head, so they judge it by what they see rather than what you see?'

'Maybe,' she said.

'I know exactly what I was feeling when you were talking to me—and you've caught it on paper.' His gaze was intense. 'Hot as hell. Desperate to be inside you.'

'That picture,' she said softly, 'would make any woman want to rip her clothes off and be with you.'

'Oh, really? Well, right now, there's only one woman I want to do that.'

He tangled his fingers with hers, shifted her gently off his lap and walked with her to the bathroom. He ran a sinkful of water and washed her hands, soaping her fingers and paying close attention to each with his thumb and forefinger. By the time he'd rinsed the suds away, dried her and rubbed the hand lotion into her skin, she was quivering.

'The way you look right now—that's just how I felt,' he said huskily, 'when you were talking to me.'

'Ah. That.' She blew out a breath. 'I keep my promises, Jake. And I'm going to follow through.'

'Are you, now?'

In answer, she peeled off her T-shirt. Stripped off the rest of her clothes in two seconds flat. Kissed him, and walked him back over to the bed. And when he was sprawled against the pillows, she smiled. 'To the letter,' she whispered.

And did so.

CHAPTER SEVEN

ON SUNDAY morning, Lydia woke in Jake's arms. Her arms were wrapped tightly round him, his thigh was caught between hers, and his cheek lay against her shoulder. She was warm and comfortable—and, the crazy thing was, it felt as if she were home, not in a hotel room hundreds of miles away from her flat in London.

She couldn't help smiling as she remembered the previous night. She had indeed made Jake see streams of light as he'd climaxed, just as she'd promised. They'd showered together, but when Jake had started arousing her she'd stopped him, wrapping her fingers round his hand and kissing his palm. 'You don't have to do this. It's not how it works.'

'Equals,' he reminded her.

'We are. But, right now,' she said, 'I'm drained.' She'd already put so much of herself into that portrait. 'And all I want to do is fall asleep in your arms.'

Exactly the way she'd woken up. Feeling secure and warm and cherished.

It would be all too easy to grow used to waking up like this. All too easy to let herself fall for Jake. Because he was everything she'd want in a partner. A generous heart, a clever mind, a gorgeous body, and a smile that made her knees go weak.

Not to mention the fantastic sex.

Though she also knew that Jake wasn't looking for a partner; he'd told her straight that he was concentrating on his career. This was an affair with very defined limits, and she wasn't going to be able to break down his barriers in a few short days. The sensible thing to do would be to put some distance between them: emotionally, and probably physically too.

Then again, this was their week out of time. And she wanted the most from every precious moment of it. So she'd go with the flow. Let herself feel. Store up memories to last her.

As if he felt her stirring, Jake turned his face slightly and pressed a kiss to her skin. She snuggled closer and his hand glided down her side, stroked over the curve of her hip and her bottom, then back up again.

'Good morning,' he said softly, his mouth skating over the sensitive spot beside her ear.

'Good morning.'

'Mmm. You smell very nice, Ms Sheridan.' He nuzzled her neck, breathing in her scent, and gently shifted her so that she was flat on her back and he was kneeling between her thighs. 'Hold that thought,' he said softly, and kissed her. Behind the heat there was a sweetness and tenderness, a weird sensation she couldn't name but she knew she'd never felt before.

As he dealt with the condom and eased into her she felt as if they were wrapped in a bubble of sheer joy.

And Lydia couldn't remember ever feeling this happy.

After breakfast—more of Jake's favourite waffles and hot chocolate, this time with out-of-season raspberries—they caught the shuttle to the airport. Jake insisted on carrying her case while she carried his briefcase.

'I'm perfectly capable of carrying my own case, Jake.'

'I know. But I'm bigger than you, and I was brought up to have good manners. So I'm carrying your case.'

There was no answer to that; she simply smiled and gave in.

The flight to Tromsø took two hours; again, Jake let her have the window seat and read the paper while she sketched. At Tromsø, even though it was late morning, it was twilight when they got off the plane—and it was snowing. Big, fat, fluffy flakes. And the ground was completely white.

'Proper snow,' she said in delight.

'It's too dry to make snowballs,' he told her, 'but I look forward to rolling you in the snow, later, and kissing you senseless.'

'Promises, promises,' she teased.

He caught her to him and kissed her, his lips teasing hers until she opened her mouth and let him deepen the kiss. When it finally ended, it took her a moment to remember just where she was.

In the middle of an airport.

With people giving them both indulgent glances as they passed—as if they were honeymooners or something.

'That's on account,' Jake said, giving her a smile of pure sin.

How he could string a sentence together, when she could barely even think coherently, was beyond her. She was speechless until after they'd boarded a bus.

'Why are we going on a bus?'

'We're in the Arctic circle, *min kjære*—a car won't make it on these roads in the winter, even with studded tyres or snow chains. And there'll be snow-blowers and a plough in front of the bus.'

Again, she sat by the window and gazed out in delight as she saw the snow piled up on the sides of the road. 'I've never, ever seen so much snow—not even in the worst winter I remember as a child. It was never really bad in London.'

'This, *elskling*, is the north. The land of snow. In April, a few years back, Tromsø still had almost two and a half metres of the stuff on the ground.'

'Two and a half metres? *In April*?' She blinked.

'It was the record snowfall, admittedly—but you normally get quite a lot of snow here.'

'It's beautiful. The fir trees look almost black against the snow.' It made her itch to sketch them, but she knew she wouldn't get a good result while they were travelling—it was too bumpy. So she curled her fingers round his and watched, entranced, until the bus stopped.

'We're staying here tonight?' she asked as Jake collected their cases and carried them in to the hotel.

'Not quite.'

Which told her nothing. 'Jake?'

'Wait and see,' he said. 'I promise you, today is an experience you won't find in many places.' He glanced at his watch. 'We have enough time for a quick lunch.'

Lunch, as she'd come to expect in Norway, involved a selection from a *koltbord*, served with good, hot coffee.

And then Jake led her to the hotel reception, where the receptionist gave him two snowsuits.

'Skiing?' Lydia asked.

'No, *min kjære*. What I have in mind is far more fun. And you don't have to do a thing.'

'I'm a lawyer. I hate surprises,' she grumbled.

'You're an artist. You love seeing new things,' he countered, and tossed the smaller snowsuit to her. 'Don't put it on here. We have another bus ride, first.'

This time, the bus ended up at what looked like a large log cabin.

Just what did he have in mind? Lydia wondered. And then, as they got off the bus, she heard barking.

Lots of barking.

And Jake had a smile on his face a mile wide. 'We're going dog sledding,' he told her. 'Yesterday was art. Today…today's the rush. Just you, me, and the frozen north. Oh, and a team of huskies.' His eyes sparkled with anticipation. 'We need to put our snowsuits on, now.' He led her into the log cabin and helped her put on the cumbersome suit.

The guide spoke, and about the only word she could recognise was *sjokolade*.

Jake translated swiftly for her. 'His name's Erik, we'll be out for about an hour, and there will be hot chocolate here to warm us up when we get back.'

Erik took them into the yard and introduced them to the dogs—white huskies with piercing blue eyes, plus some smaller black Norwegian huskies. The dogs were all bright-eyed with madly wagging tails, and were clearly very happy to be there, and Lydia was enchanted by them.

'Do you speak English, please?' she asked Erik.

'I do. I'm sorry, I thought everyone today was from Norway, or I would have come over to tell you the itinerary in English.'

'It's not a problem. Jake translated for me so I know what's happening,' she reassured him. 'I was just wondering…may I make a fuss of the dogs, *vær så snill*?'

Erik looked delighted that she'd made the effort to say 'please' in his language. 'Of course.'

She crouched down and petted the dogs, who responded by wagging their tails even harder.

'I didn't think to ask, so it's just as well you're not scared of dogs,' Jake said, looking slightly guilty. 'Do you have a dog at home?'

'Emma does—a soppy black Labrador called Monty.' Lydia lifted one shoulder in a half-shrug. 'I would've liked a dog when I was younger, but my parents weren't keen. Too messy, and they didn't have time to take the dog out for walks.'

'We've always had dogs,' Jake said. 'My grandparents have two Norwegian Elkhounds. The original Viking war dogs.'

'War dogs?' she repeated, shocked.

'It's not as bad as it sounds.' He laughed. 'They make a lot of noise, so they sound scary, and they're incredibly inquisitive…but they're soft as butter. And my mother has two Westies, Poppy and Woody, which are incredibly spoiled.'

Mmm, and she could guess just who spoiled them most.

Once their team of eight dogs was harnessed, Jake helped her into the sled and tucked her in with furs.

'You're going in a separate sled?' she asked.

'No, *elskling*, I'm driving this one.'

She blinked. 'You can drive a sled?'

He smiled. 'It's been a while, but it's like riding

a bike—you don't forget how to do it. You'll be perfectly safe with me.'

She believed him. Because, with Jake, she somehow felt...protected.

They went in single file, with Erik in the first sled and three others behind them. As they raced along the smooth path in the snow it felt like flying. And it was like travelling through a fairy-tale land, with fir trees and snow and the unbelievable whiteness and freshness around them; the trees looked almost like ghosts in the darkening light, and somehow the snow managed to sparkle like diamonds at the same time.

Their path took them over crisp fresh snow and frozen rivers, and even the weather was on their side because, although the clouds didn't break, the snow had stopped falling. Just as well, Lydia thought, because they were going so fast that any snow would've stung her face, and the air was so cold that it tasted metallic.

And she wouldn't have missed a single second of this.

All the while she was aware of Jake behind her, steady and strong and knowing exactly what he was doing, in perfect control of the dogs. Like the Viking explorer she'd teased him about being in the ship museum.

With a man like Jake by her side, she'd be afraid of nothing.

And he wouldn't have taken her father's cheque.

Except maybe to tear it into tiny pieces and scatter it like confetti.

Afterwards, back at the log cabin, Jake asked, 'Did you enjoy it?'

'It was fantastic—like being in a winter wonderland.'

He brushed a kiss against her mouth, then helped her out of her snowsuit.

They warmed up with a mug of hot chocolate, and Lydia felt as if she were glowing from the inside. 'That was an incredible way to get rid of the cobwebs. Thank you.'

'My pleasure, *elskling*.' Though the sparkle in his eyes told her that he'd enjoyed it just as much as she had.

By the time they returned to the hotel, it was dark and the temperature had dropped even lower.

'Cold?' Jake asked when she shivered.

'A little bit,' she admitted.

'You know the best thing we can do to warm up?'

Oh, yes. She felt her skin heat. 'We have a room?'

He laughed. 'Not here, we don't. Actually, I meant a sauna. Or we could go for a hot tub.'

'A hot tub sounds fantastic. Unless…it's not outdoors, is it?'

'No, but there's a glass roof. We might be lucky and see the Lights, if the clouds decide to clear. Though don't pin your hopes on it, *min kjære*.'

They were the only ones in the hot tub, and the

bubbling water felt fantastic against her skin, warming her through. To her disappointment, the cloud cover stayed put; there was no chance of seeing the Northern Lights. So instead she watched Jake.

With his eyes closed and his head tipped back against the rim of the hot tub, he looked utterly blissful; she'd remember that image later, and sketch him.

'This is the second-best way I know of making sure your muscles don't seize up,' he said.

'The first being a sauna followed by a plunge into ice-cold water?' she teased.

'No, the first being making sure you're in shape before you drive a sled. I'm glad my regular workout uses a rowing machine.' He smiled. 'But if I hurt, it's my own fault for showing off.' Then he opened his eyes and looked straight at her. 'Though there are other ways to stay in shape. And if it's a choice between going to the gym, or having hot sex with a woman who intrigues my mind as well as thrilling my body…' He moistened his lower lip. 'Well, that's a no-brainer.'

He could've been describing the way she felt about him. A man who intrigued her mind and thrilled her body.

So was he saying that this week might not have limits, after all?

She blew out a breath. 'Are you sure we don't have a room here?'

'Patience, *elskling*,' he said, giving her a slow, sensual smile. 'And we need to get out of here anyway, before we look like prunes.'

When they'd dried off and dressed, Jake took her for dinner in the hotel restaurant. 'Do you mind if I order for you?' he asked. 'As we're in the Arctic Circle, I'd recommend trying the local delicacies. As long as you're OK with seafood, that is.'

He ordered grilled king crab on a bed of avocado purée—the most tender and melting seafood she'd ever eaten—followed by salmon, and then a cold pudding that tasted of almonds served with a hot blueberry compote.

'I could definitely get used to Arctic specialities,' she said when she'd finished. 'The food's fantastic.'

Though the company was even better.

They lingered over coffee; then Jake glanced at his watch. 'Time to go.'

'Go where?' she asked, mystified.

He led her to the reception area. 'We're storing our luggage here overnight,' he said. 'We just need a small bag with the essentials.'

'We're spending the night outside to see the Northern Lights?' she guessed.

He indicated the sky. 'It's unlikely that this cloud cover will go, *min kjære*, so we wouldn't see a thing and would probably freeze. But it's something I hope you'll enjoy. Something special.'

Once they'd sorted their luggage, they joined a

small group of people to be taken out across the snow by snowmobile taxi. And at their destination, the sign—presented in a carved block of ice—told her exactly where they were.

'We're spending the night in an ice hotel?'

'You were saying about winter wonderlands, earlier. This would be the fairy palace,' Jake said.

She felt her eyes widening as they were shown around the hotel. Every room had a different design, with sculptures ranging from chessboards to dragons and trolls and horses, and all were lit with different colour schemes—lavender, turquoise, and apricot—with the lights encased in the ice.

'This is amazing,' she said. Jake simply smiled.

'How come the heat from the lights isn't melting the ice?'

'Clever construction and fibre optics,' was all he said.

In the middle of their room was a large bed, carved from clear blocks of ice, in the shape of a sleigh being pulled by wild horses; there was a proper mattress in the middle of the bed, with reindeer skins on top.

'We'll give you a sleeping bag before you come here,' their guide said, 'and it's best to stuff your outdoor clothing at the bottom of the sleeping bag, so it will be comfortable to put on again in the morning. Leave it out, and it'll be a little cold.'

Lydia had a feeling that was an understatement. 'How cold is it in here?' she asked.

'Between minus four and minus six Celsius.' The guide smiled. 'Otherwise it would melt. But the restrooms outside the ice hotel are warm.'

'Minus four,' she repeated.

'It's warmer than it is outside. And it's surprisingly comfortable, as long as you remember not to breathe into your sleeping bag—if you do, you'll get damp and cold,' the guide said. 'But you'll wake feeling refreshed.'

Lydia decided to reserve judgement. But she knew that Jake had planned this as a special treat, and she didn't want him to feel that she was throwing it back in his face, so she smiled.

Besides, the architecture was so stunning, it took her mind off the temperature.

Their room felt almost like a cathedral made from ice, with fan vaulting soaring upwards and a tiny 'rose' window high in one wall, lit by a turquoise light. 'I've never seen anything so beautiful,' she said. 'The architecture is incredible, and the sheer amount of work that goes into creating a place of magic like this…'

'Especially when you remember that it melts every spring and they build it from the ground up every winter,' Jake added. 'Artists queue up for the privilege of designing a room here.'

'If I sculpted,' she said, 'I'd want to do this, too. How does the story go?' She cast her mind back to the story that had fascinated her as a child. '"The walls of the Snow Queen's castle were made of drifting snow, and the doors and windows of piercing winds." But this is much more beautiful.'

'And you, *min kjære*, are rather nicer than the Snow Queen. Though I won't object if you want to make me forget everything with a kiss, later,' he added with a smile. 'I'm glad you like it. Let's have another wander round; then we can have a drink in the bar.'

The bar was a real showpiece, with sculptures of swans and polar bears and reindeer; the ice in the sculptures was perfectly clear, but lit with the same turquoise colour as the one in their room. The chairs and tables were also made out of ice, though there were reindeer skins on the chair seats to protect people from the cold. There was a sculptured fountain, too, carved from ice and with drops of water seemingly frozen in mid-flow, the carving as delicate and brittle as a spider's web covered in frost.

'I'm afraid it's a choice of a spirit-based drink or a spirit-based drink,' Jake said as they reached the counter, 'because anything else would freeze.'

Lydia chose a vanilla-flavoured vodka while he opted for a blue-coloured concoction. Their glasses were made from ice, a crystal-clear cube with a cylinder bored through it; to her delight, hers also had a flower frozen into the base. 'Now there's a touch of the exotic.' She sipped her drink. 'Mmm, and so's this.' It was the most warming, lovely thing she'd ever tasted: smoother than she'd expected, with just enough sweetness to take away the burn of the spirit without being sickly. The scent, too, was gorgeous and added to the feeling of warmth. 'I think I could get a taste for vanilla-flavoured vodka. So is this the first time you've stayed at an ice hotel?'

'Yes. But it's something I've always wanted to do.' He laced his gloved fingers through hers. 'And I'm glad I'm sharing it with you.'

She was glad, too. Jake was making this week so special for her. Showing her the wonders of life…and crystallising her feelings about exactly where she wanted her life to go, from here on.

When it was time to go to bed, Jake collected the large double sleeping bag from their changing room. 'It's a subzero sleeping bag—apparently, it will work for temperatures up to minus thirty Celsius, so we just need to wear socks, thermal underwear and a hat.'

'You told me you could make thermal underwear sexy.' She raised an eyebrow. 'I didn't believe you.'

'I haven't…*yet*,' Jake said.

The heat in his eyes made desire shimmer all the way down her spine.

Quickly, they changed out of their clothes, stuffed them in the bottom of the sleeping bag as they'd been told, and went through the woollen curtain that served as a door to their suite. Jake dimmed the lights and unzipped the sleeping bag.

'What I can't get over,' Lydia said as he wriggled

into the sleeping bag beside her and pulled up the zip, 'is how quiet it is.'

'The ice and the snow deaden the sound,' he explained. 'So nobody's going to disturb us. Now, this thing about thermal underwear...' He slid one hand under the hem of her vest, stroking her abdomen. 'It's too cold for me to take all your clothes off and kiss you all over, the way I'd like to—we'd both freeze.'

Yeah. He could say that again. *Minus four.*

'So I need to do this with your clothes on. I can't see what I'm doing: just touch you. Unwrap the layers, yet keep you wrapped at the same time.' His fingers slid a little further north, and his thumb found her hardening nipple. 'Like this,' he whispered.

'We're going to...here?'

'No, *elskling.* I'm just going to touch you. Relax you.'

'Relax?' Not quite the word she'd use to describe the way she felt when he touched her.

'Well, you'll relax afterwards. Close your eyes,' he directed softly. 'Concentrate on the way I'm making you feel.'

His touch was slow and leisurely, light as a snowflake, and Lydia felt herself growing hotter and hotter as his thumb and forefinger teased her nipples. When his hand slid down over her abdomen, she parted her thigh, welcoming his touch; she was already wet for him, and so desperate for him to touch her.

He eased one finger into her, then found just the right spot with his thumb; he circled and teased her until she was quivering, completely incoherent.

'Open your eyes now, *elskling*,' he whispered.

She did—and in the darkness, she could see the tiny rose window, the turquoise light glowing across the roof of snow and filling her head. The light seemed to ripple in tune with her body, little shocks of pleasure radiating out and joining together until her climax slammed into her.

'Jake.' Ignoring the cold, ignoring everything, she cupped his face in her hands and kissed him deeply.

He'd taken her practically to the ends of the earth, in the Arctic Circle. And, here, he'd shown her pleasure like she'd had no idea existed.

When the aftershocks of her climax died away, Jake shifted so that he was lying on his back and holding her close, her head pillowed on his shoulder and her arm draped across him.

Lydia slipped her fingers under the hem of his thermal vest, and he laid his free hand over hers, stilling it.

'Jake…'

'Consider it payback from last night,' he said softly. 'Or, if you really want to do something for me…' He paused.

'Yes?'

'Tell me,' he said, 'why someone who's such a good artist is burying her talent and working as a lawyer.'

CHAPTER EIGHT

'It's a long story.'

'I'm not going anywhere.' Jake pressed a light kiss against Lydia's forehead. 'Tell me, *elskling*.'

'My parents…' How could she tell him that her parents hadn't wanted her? That she'd been a mistake—and compounded that mistake in their eyes by being a girl rather than a boy.

And even saying it sounded whiny. It made her feel like a spoilt child stamping her foot because she couldn't get her own way. 'It doesn't matter.'

He drew her closer. 'I think it does. Or you wouldn't be locking yourself away like this. You were saying: your parents?'

She sighed. 'They had my best interests at heart.' She'd been telling herself that for years. 'I mean, artists are ten a penny. And I could spend years working hard and getting nowhere, not even earning enough to live on. Starving in a garret. Whereas if I followed them into law, I'd always have a steady job and I wouldn't have to worry about where I was going to find the next payment for my rent. And they were absolutely right. I have a steady, fulfilling job and no financial worries.'

'And you hate it.'

'I don't *hate* it, exactly.'

'But you're not happy. There's something missing.'

She couldn't deny that. 'Maybe,' she hedged.

'All right. Let me ask you this. If you had the chance to do it all again, would you do anything differently?'

She nodded—and then realised how ridiculous it was. There wasn't enough light for him to see her. 'Yes,' she said softly. 'I would've done Art instead of Economics. And I would've gone to art school.'

'Your art teacher must've been able to see how talented you were. So why didn't your teacher step in and fight your corner?'

'She tried. My father's quite…' How could she put this? 'Formidable.'

'Was he violent towards you?' Jake's voice sounded cool and neutral, but at the same time his hold on her tightened. Telling her that he was furious on her behalf, wanted to protect her.

'No, not that.' The blows her father had used hadn't been physical. The scars they'd left were invisible, and she'd never spoken about them. 'Just that it's very rare for my father to lose an argument—in court or outside. He's very good with words.' She sighed. 'And yes, I know I probably should've stood up to him and followed my heart.

But I was young and I'd always been pretty much sheltered.' And her father had discouraged her wilder friends, making very sure that it was inconvenient for her to go out with them.

'And maybe where other teenagers rebelled against their parents, I just wanted mine to be proud of me.' She'd needed to hear the words 'well done'. Needed the proud smile, the quick hug, the softness in their eyes. And she'd so wanted to prove that she could live up to their expectations—that she was better than the son she knew they would rather have had.

'Why would you think they weren't proud of you?'

Because it was so obvious.

And how pathetic that sounded. She didn't need other people to validate her. She *knew* that. So she aimed for a casual tone. 'It's not important. I'm over this, Jake.'

'You're not, or you'd be able to talk about it.'

Trust him to get straight to the heart of the matter. Well, when he'd talked to her, she hadn't let him off the hook. She'd made him say the words out loud, knowing that he needed to get the feelings out before they corroded him.

And now he was returning the compliment.

No pain, no gain. 'They have…high standards.'

'How high?' he asked gently. 'I've seen your file, remember. You were a straight-A student. You can't get any better than that, Lydia.'

'Percentage-wise, you can.' The words slid out

before she could stop them. Words she'd never, ever said to anyone before.

'Percentage-wise?'

She bit her lip. 'Doesn't matter.'

'Tell me.'

She said nothing.

But neither did he.

And eventually the silence pushed it out of her. 'Every time I came home after a test or what have you, and my father asked how I'd done, and I told him I'd come top of the class, he wanted to know my percentage. Then he'd ask where I'd made the mistakes— what had stopped me getting one hundred per cent.'

Jake muttered something in Norwegian that she couldn't translate, but from the tone of his voice she guessed he was swearing. And that wasn't fair. 'He wanted me to do my best. So it made me work harder, Jake. That's why I did well in my exams, because he pushed me to be as good as I could be.'

'No. It's why you underestimate yourself, Lydia. Because you see yourself through your father's perfectionist eyes, and you see a failure.'

'I know I'm not a failure. But I'm realistic about it. I do my job well, but only up to a point. I don't have the hunger to be really brilliant.'

'Not the hunger for law, maybe. But there's your art.'

'I'm not sure I have the hunger to be brilliant at that, either. Otherwise surely I would've done it earlier?'

'How, when you were constantly being told that what you wanted was worthless?'

She had no answer to that.

'I can't believe he said that artists were ten a penny.' Jake sounded really shocked. 'Artists with your kind of talent really aren't that common. And if you hadn't wanted to take the fine art route, there were all sorts of things you could've done. If financial security was so important, you could've gone into advertising—you could've been the art director at a big agency.'

The best of both worlds.

She'd *almost*, almost taken that step.

Until Robbie. And then her new-found confidence had vanished again. The slap of rejection had knocked her back.

And that was something she really couldn't tell Jake about. Because she was way, way too ashamed of being so weak and needy.

'What about your mother? She must've seen how good you are. Why didn't she tell your father to give you a chance?'

Now that one she could answer. 'Because she agreed with him.' Her parents had always, but always, had a united front.

Jake stroked her hair. 'It sounds to me as if your parents never saw who you were or asked you what you wanted. And they pushed you into following their career.'

'Not quite. My father works in criminal law and my mother works in family law.' Which made her choice just different enough to be her own. 'And it was a point of pride, too. I wanted to prove to myself that I could do it.' She paused. 'Anyway, you're working in the family firm. I bet your parents expected you to do it.'

'Yes,' Jake said, 'but it wasn't an issue because that was exactly what I wanted to do, right from when I was small and went out in the boat with Dad and *Farfar*. And I know my parents would've supported my decision if I'd decided to do something else with my life—they'd have talked it over with me, helped me work out the pros and cons so I made the right decision for me, and then backed me all the way.'

'How can you be so sure about that?' It was so far from her own experience that she couldn't quite get her head round it.

'Put it this way: Dad moved Andersen's from Trondheim to London, to be with Mum, and my grandfather didn't give him a hard time about it. *Farfar* and *Farmor* backed his decision, just as my parents would back me. The only thing Dad insisted on was that I should spend time in each department during my university holidays and for the first couple of years after I graduated, and work from the bottom up so I could understand what everyone did. Including cleaning the office and scrubbing barnacles off a boat. He said you can't lead a business properly unless you know exactly how it's put together and what makes it work and what kind of problems your staff face—and he was absolutely right about that. I respect his judgement. He wouldn't ask anything of me that he wouldn't ask of himself.'

'My father expects high standards of himself, too,' Lydia pointed out. 'He was one of the youngest QCs ever.'

'I can imagine the hours he put in to achieve that. But, when you have children, you need to find a balance between your work and your family. You have to make time for them, too,' Jake said softly. 'Would I be right in guessing that your parents never made it to your nativity play or sports day, when you were little?'

She sucked in a breath. 'They were busy.'

'Of course they were. But, as I said, even when you're busy you still have to find a balance. Although my father ran an international company, he made time to help me make a shepherd's crook for my nativity play when I was six. And he'd re-schedule a meeting rather than miss me doing something at school, whether it was an egg-and-spoon race or a rugby match,' Jake said.

Because Jake's parents clearly loved him to bits. She swallowed the bile that rose from her stomach. 'They were there for the important things. My graduation.'

'I think I understand now why you're not as close to your family as I am to mine, *min kjære.*'

No, he didn't. He didn't understand at all. She wanted to be close to them: but she knew that they didn't feel the same way about her. So she'd put some emotional distance between them to stop it hurting so much. Pushed them away before they could reject her yet again.

'Your godmother, Polly. You said she's a designer. And she's your mother's best friend. Didn't she take your side and tell them how talented you were?'

'She had a fairly huge row with my parents over it,' Lydia admitted. 'They didn't speak for months. But then she took me out to lunch and told me that she was going to try a softly-softly approach—I could sketch at her place, keep my art stuff there, and tell my parents that I'd given it up completely so they didn't nag me about it. I felt bad about lying, but at least it stopped all the rows and the atmosphere.'

'So you've been hiding your talent for almost half a lifetime.'

'I already told you. I'm a coward.'

'Lydia, you need to remember that you can't please all of the people, all of the time.'

He didn't say it, but she knew he was thinking it. Just as she was. Where her parents were concerned, she couldn't please any of the people, any of the time.

'Maybe,' he said quietly, 'it's time to stop trying so hard. Stop hiding. Be who you want to be.'

She sighed. 'You have a point. It's been really nagging at me, this year. I guess you're right about everything changing when you hit thirty. It's made me reassess my life, think about what I really want.' And she really wanted to stop talking about herself.

'What about you, Jake? Who do you want to be?'

'I'm comfortable in my own skin.'

She wasn't so sure. 'In Oslo, you said you were at a crossroads.'

'I was. But you've put things into perspective for me—showing you round, these last couple of days, has reminded me what it's like to feel, instead of shutting myself off. And I love Andersen Marine. I really, really love my job. So, actually, I'm quite happy as I am. All I needed was a bit of perspective to make me realise that.' He twisted slightly so he could kiss her lightly. 'I'm fine, *elskling*. And thank you for helping.'

'No problem. And you've helped me. I know what I'm going to do, when I'm back in England. Be brave. And, um, I think you might need to find another lawyer.'

'I still think you're a good lawyer. You picked things up in that contract with Nils that I missed, and I thought I was pretty sharp-eyed. But I'm not going to stand in your way. I said if you still wanted to resign, after you'd worked with me on this contract, I'd let you do it and I keep my promises.'

'Thank you.'

'Now, let's get some sleep.' He kept his arms wrapped round her. 'And just remember, Lydia, you're a damn sight better than you believe you are.'

They were woken the next morning by one of the staff bringing hot lingonberry juice; the drink was tart, refreshing and very warming. Lydia's head felt clearer than it had for years, and her heart felt lighter, too.

'Did you sleep all right?' Jake asked.

'Surprisingly well,' she admitted. 'I wasn't cold at all.' Because she'd been wrapped in his arms all night long. *Cherished.* And the warmth of that could've carried her through the night even if the temperature had dropped another twenty degrees Celsius.

'So how are you feeling?' he asked.

'Great.' She kissed him lingeringly. 'And you're wonderful, do you know that? Thanks for…well, listening, last night.'

'I'm glad it helped,' he said lightly.

'It did.' To the point where she felt that she knew exactly who she was. And she wasn't scared any more. She was looking forward to the future—and finally she could relax with Jake, enjoy this crazy fling for what it was. 'So what's on the agenda today?'

'Back to the Paris of the North. Tromsø,' he added at her questioning look. 'We'll still be within the Arctic Circle, so there's still a chance we might see the Northern Lights. I did think about taking you to see the polar bears.' He spread his hands. 'The problem is, Svalbard is the best place to see them, and it's really far north; it takes almost as long to fly to Longyearbyen from here as it does to Oslo, and at this time of year whatever time we get there it'll be dark.'

'So we won't be able to see much.'

'Exactly. You'd be better off coming back in the summer and going by boat—and you're more likely to see polar bear cubs then, too.'

She noted he said 'you' rather than 'we', but pushed the regret away. They had this week. To ask for more would be…needy.

And she wasn't weak and needy. Not any more. Not the way she'd been when she'd met Robbie.

'I might just do that,' she said.

'Come on. Let's go and warm up properly.'

They made a dash for their changing room, dressed swiftly, and took the bus back to the hotel. It had snowed again in the night, but the skies were clear and the snow sparkled in the blue light of the polar winter day, and the temperature was definitely lower than had it been inside the ice hotel.

'This is completely the wrong way round,' Jake said in exasperation. 'We're meant to have cloudy days and then nice clear nights.'

She laughed. 'I know your organisational skills are legendary, Jake, but even you can't tell the weather what to do.'

He laughed back. 'Yeah. I suppose. Maybe we'll be lucky tonight.'

Back at the hotel, they had breakfast; the hot coffee helped to warm her.

Jake touched her cheek. 'You still feel a bit cold. A sauna might help.'

'I'll pass, thanks.' Chilly or not, she'd rather spend the time with him. Not that she was going to put any pressure on him by saying that. 'But if you want one, feel free.'

He shook his head. 'There's a bus back to Tromsø in about fifteen minutes.'

'You want to make the most of the daylight?' she asked.

'Absolutely. It'll be dark by mid-afternoon.'

The city was set partly on an island, joined by a bridge to the mainland. Jake either knew the city, or had read up about it, because he'd found a couple of places to visit once they'd dropped their luggage off at their hotel. She loved the clean lines and angles of the Arctic Cathedral, a spectacular white building shaped like an iceberg, but when she tried sketching with her gloves on she couldn't get the kind of detail she wanted.

'Don't be tempted, because you'll end up with frostbite,' Jake said.

She knew he was right, so she took photos instead, jamming her hands into her pockets afterwards for extra warmth.

They wandered around the shops and ate that night at a restaurant overlooking the harbour. Although she kept looking out to sea, hoping to see a flash of green in the sky, the clouds rolled in and it started to snow again.

'Maybe tomorrow,' Jake said ruefully.

'Maybe.' On the way back to their hotel, she stopped underneath a streetlamp.

'What?'

'Just this.' She slid her arms round his neck, drew her head down to his and kissed him, tiny nibbling kisses that teased and tormented and coaxed until he opened his mouth, letting her deepen the kiss. The air was cold against her face but she didn't care; all she could focus on was the heat of his mouth.

'That,' he said, when she finally broke the kiss, 'was wonderful. But may I ask why?'

'Cold snow, hot man. It's a nice contrast.' Plus she had a picture in her head. The snow falling like stars onto Jake's dark hair.

He gave her a slow, sensual smile. 'I'm tempted to tip you into the next snowdrift. Except we'd get arrested for public indecency. And what I need to do with you right now is—'

She pressed the tip of her gloved forefinger lightly against his lips. 'Jake. Stop talking and take me to bed.'

His response was a hot, sweet kiss that had her blood tingling all the way back to their hotel room.

At the door, Jake paused. 'I know you still haven't seen the Northern Lights in the sky. But tonight I'm going to make you see them in your head. Starting now.' He picked her up, carried her into their room, and kicked the door shut behind him.

CHAPTER NINE

ON TUESDAY, they flew south to Bodø. 'We're still in with a chance of seeing the lights,' Jake told Lydia, 'even though we're heading south. And this is a really quick stopover. There's something I want to show you.' In the city, he checked the tide time-tables, then hired a taxi to take them out to the Skjer-stad fjord. He led Lydia down to the viewing area.

'Watch and wait,' he said. 'Any minute now.'

Though he watched Lydia's face rather than the spectacle that he knew was about to unfold, and he enjoyed seeing her expression of wonder as the smooth water started forming tiny eddies that suddenly spun together, making a huge whirlpool stretching into the narrow strait.

'It's the Saltstraumen, the world's strongest mael-strom. It happens every six hours when the tide changes. All that energy's amazing—four hundred million tons of water shifting at around twenty-two knots—and yet you can sail through it.'

'You're kidding!'

'There's a window where it's relatively safe to sail through the sound. It's a fisherman's paradise. Lawrence—my best friend—and I came here after we graduated.' He smiled at the memories. 'We sailed from here to the Lofoten islands and watched the sea eagles. It's a good place to be in summer.'

'Less windy?' she asked wryly.

He laughed. 'Tromsø's the Paris of the north, so I guess Bodø's the Chicago. The windy city.' He looped his arm round her waist. 'We went diving here, too. On the rock faces below the whirlpools, there are corals and sea lilies. They're stunning.'

She glanced out at the turbulent water. 'Isn't it dangerous to dive out here?'

'Not if you take the proper safety precautions and dive in controlled circumstances. We had a ball.' He laughed, remembering. 'It was a great trip. Mind you, Lawrence was pretty spooked when we saw the fata morgana, one morning.'

'The fata morgana?'

'It's a mirage—you know how people see pools of water in the desert? On the sea, it's inverted, so you see islands and ice floating above the horizon rather than below it. I admit, they're a bit eerie—especially on a still Arctic morning.'

'You really love the north, don't you?'

'Yes.'

She pressed a kiss to the corner of his mouth. 'And yet the good memories are making you sad I can see it in your eyes. What's wrong, Jake? You fell out with Lawrence?'

'No.' But he knew he'd been avoiding his best friend. And his godchildren. Until his stay in hospital, Jake had enjoyed spending time with the kids, making a fuss of them and building railway tracks for Josh and towers for Maisie to knock down. But since the operation, he'd made excuse after excuse not to go and visit. He hated himself for hurting Lawrence and Mandy by pushing them away—but it was just too raw. He found it too hard to see what Lawrence had, knowing that he wanted the same for himself and it wasn't going to happen.

'OK, so you don't want to talk about it,' she said, clearly seeing the set expression on his face. 'I'll give you some advice instead.'

He frowned. 'What sort of advice?'

'Try being a little kinder to yourself.'

'Like you are?'

'Like I'm going to be,' she said.

The taxi took them back to Bodø, and they flew further south to Trondheim.

'This used to be the capital of Norway. The king of Norway has been crowned here for two thousand years,' Jake said reflectively. 'The name means "nice place to live"—and it is.'

'You know it well?' she asked.

'My grandparents live near here, so I've spent a fair bit of time here. It's too dark and too late to go sightseeing now, but we'll have dinner and at least we'll have a full day here tomorrow,' he said.

During dinner, Jake said softly, 'You're fidgety, this evening.'

'Sorry.'

'You're itching to paint, aren't you?'

She gave him a surprised look. 'How do you know?'

'Because you look how I feel when I've taken time off—raring to get going again.'

She stilled. 'Do you want to go back to England now?'

Part of him wanted to answer yes. Because, despite their agreement not to get involved, he knew he was falling for Lydia.

He liked the quickness of her mind. Her shy smile. The wonder in her eyes when he touched her. The softness of her skin.

And it wasn't fair to do this to her. He couldn't fall in love with her. Couldn't ask her to share his life. Even if they could get round the issue that he knew she wanted children and he couldn't have them, there was also the fact that he didn't know how long he'd stay in remission.

In sickness and in health.

The words echoed in his head. How could he possibly saddle her with a vow like that, knowing that it was more likely to be sickness?

Plus she was on the cusp of changing her life, of finally doing what she'd always wanted to do instead of burying herself in her job. She didn't need the added complication of a relationship. She'd said herself that she wasn't looking for a relationship right now.

Although he knew she was as attracted to him as he was to her, he had no idea what was going on in her head. How she felt about him. He could ask her, but he wasn't sure he'd get a completely honest answer; she'd spent half her life hiding who she was, so how could he expect her to let her guard down with him completely after only a few short days?

He hadn't been completely honest with her, either. He hadn't told her about the thing that had blown his life apart. She'd told him her demons, but he hadn't trusted her with his. And the longer he left it, the harder it was to say.

'No, I don't want to go back to England, yet. Apart from the fact that we haven't managed to see the Northern Lights, we still have a couple of days left. Let's go back to the hotel. You can paint and I'll read for a bit,' he said, trying his best to sound casual.

'Sure?'

'Sure.'

Back at the hotel, he picked up a book, but he couldn't concentrate on the words.

Because he couldn't get Lydia out of his head.

In the end he watched her working. When she

concentrated, the tip of her tongue was caught between her teeth. And he'd just bet she had no idea how cute she looked.

His heart contracted as he imagined a little girl concentrating on a drawing. A little girl with Lydia's smile and his own eyes. Or a little boy with Lydia's dark eyes and his own unruly hair.

Ah, hell.

It wasn't going to happen, so why torture himself with wishes of what might have been?

All the same, he couldn't take his eyes off her. And every single fibre of his being wanted her. Wanted it all.

She looked up and met his gaze. 'I thought you were reading?'

'I'm relaxing,' he said, forcing a smile he didn't feel. 'How's it going?'

'Want to see?'

'I'd love to.'

She'd been painting the maelstrom, and he was amazed at how she'd caught the sheer force of the water as it surged through the sound, the blueness of the water. 'I can just imagine myself back there—I can almost hear the noise of the wind and the current.'

'Good. That's what you're supposed to do.' She smiled. 'Well, I'm done for now.' She put her pastels away and cleaned up; when she came out of the bathroom, she said softly, 'You've been brooding all evening. You listened to me: it's my turn to listen to you.'

Yes, he'd been brooding. But he had no intention of explaining what was in his head. He didn't want her to run a mile, the way Grace had. 'I'm fine.'

'No, you're not.'

She was right, but it was way too difficult to explain. 'Do me a favour?' he asked.

'Sure.'

'Come here.' He held his arms open.

She looked torn—as if she knew he needed physical comfort and wanted to give it to him, but also as if she thought it wouldn't fix the problem.

Of course it wouldn't. Nothing could.

'Right now,' he said softly, 'I just want to be close to you.'

How could she resist those words? Or the light in those gorgeous blue eyes?

She walked over towards him. Let him haul her onto his lap and wrap his arms round her. He kissed her, his mouth sweet and inviting, and then desire flared between them, burning all thoughts from her head, all she could do was feel.

She wasn't aware of when they'd removed their clothes—or how—but the next thing she knew she was lying back against cool, smooth cotton sheets, and Jake was kissing his way down her body, nuzzling the valley between her breasts.

'Gardenia. I love that scent.'

Love.

She felt as if someone had just doused her in water straight from one of the fjords.

Love.

She couldn't possibly have fallen in love with Jake. Not this fast.

And yet that was the word in her head. Love. Because Jake was everything she wanted. The complete opposite of what the men in her life had been so far. Decent and honourable, unlike Robbie. Warm and caring, and interested in her for who she was, not for who he wanted her to be.

He'd made it clear that he wasn't in the market for a relationship, so she wasn't going to say the words out loud. She wasn't going to break their deal and ask for more.

But she'd tell him in her head.

I love you.

Her hands fisted in his hair as he moved lower, drew a circle round her navel with the tip of his tongue. She arched her back as he moved lower still, quivered as he stroked her thighs apart, and gave herself up to pleasure at the first long, slow stroke of his tongue. Every touch, every kiss, stoked her desire higher.

Why had she been so naïve as to think that this week of stolen pleasure would slake her desire for him, get it out of her system? If anything, it seemed to have driven the need for him deeper into her soul.

'Jake,' she whispered. 'I need you inside me. Now.'

He kissed his way back up her body. 'Your wish is my command, *elskling*,' he murmured into her ear, and nudged her thighs wider apart. Slowly, gently, he eased inside her.

It felt like coming home.

Belonging.

And the wave of sensation almost swamped her. She needed to be back in control. Fast.

'Jake.'

'Mmm?' He looked slightly dazed.

Was it the same for him?

She didn't dare hope. Couldn't face the kind of rejection she'd had before.

'Roll over,' she said softly. 'I want to…'

He stroked her face. 'You want to be in charge?'

She felt her skin heat. 'I'm sorry.'

'Hey. It's fine.' He gave her a slow, sensual smile. 'More than fine. Do with me what you will.'

If only she could take him up on that.

But then he rolled over onto his back, taking her with him and staying inside her. She shifted her position slightly, pushing him back against the pillows before moving over him. Jake twined his fingers through hers, his hold tightening as his arousal grew. She could hear his breathing growing faster and shallower; at the same time, she could feel pleasure gathering inside her and beginning to radiate outward.

As she stopped moving Jake loosened her hands, sat up and wrapped his arms tightly round her. She clung to him for support, her gaze locked with his, and watched his eyes go glassy as he hit his climax, half a second before her own rocked through her and she gasped, burying her face in his shoulder.

I love you, she thought.

I love you.

Wednesday turned out to be a bright, sunny day. 'We're still getting the days and nights mixed up,' Jake grumbled.

'Does the aurora ever appear before dawn?'

'No. The aurora zone here is from six in the evening until about midnight.' He spread his hands. 'It's infuriating. Still. Let's make the most of the sunshine.' After an early breakfast of coffee, fruit and yoghurt, Jake showed Lydia round Trondheim. It was a small, intimate city centre with wide streets, and she loved it.

There was a statue on a huge pedestal in the middle of the town square, wearing a pointed helmet and carrying a sword in one hand and a beacon in the other. 'Who's that?' she asked.

'Olav Tryggvason, the Viking king. It's also the world's largest sundial,' Jake explained, showing her the markings round its base. 'Does he remind you of anyone?'

She glanced at Jake; she could imagine him as a

Viking king, standing in the prow of his boat. 'One of your ancestors?' she hazarded.

Jake chuckled. 'I doubt it. No, he reminds me of the Lewis chessmen. It's thought that they might have been made here in Trondheim.'

'Now you've pointed it out, I can see the resemblance.'

'Come on. I want to show you the old part of the town.' He walked hand in hand with her across Gamle Bybro, the old town bridge that stretched over the river Nidelva. 'This is Bakklandet. And, if you'll forgive the pun, it's right up your street.'

He was right. She loved window-shopping in the art galleries and antique shops, seeing the old wooden houses painted in different colours.

'It's really pretty in the summer, when you can see the cobbles in the streets.'

Cobbles that were currently covered with a layer of snow; even as she thought it she found herself slipping, but Jake caught her before she fell.

'OK?' he asked.

'Fine.' She smiled back at him. With him by her side, strong and reliable, she was more than fine. She just had to remember that this was temporary. 'Thanks for rescuing me.'

There was an unfathomable expression in his eyes as he replied, *'Vær så god.'*

Was he warning her that she was getting too close?

Ha. He was way too late.

So she'd just have to learn to un-fall in love with him.

Jake found them a table at a café overlooking the water at lunchtime, knowing that Lydia would love the sight of the reflections of the wharf in the river; as he'd half expected, when he came back from ordering their meal he could see her taking photographs. And it was as if she were lit up from the inside; right now, he was seeing the real Lydia. The one she'd kept hidden from everyone.

He needed to take this carefully, make sure he didn't rush her and scare her back into her shell. So he kept the conversation light and casual over lunch.

She was entranced by what he'd always thought as Trondheim's most beautiful building, the gothic splendour of Nidarosdomen Cathedral.

'The rose window is just stunning,' she whispered as they looked up at it. 'The colours—' rich ruby reds and deep blues and purples '—and the shapes; I can imagine Polly being inspired to design a silk scarf or something based round that. She'd adore this.'

'You're close to her, aren't you?' he asked softly.

Lydia shrugged. 'She's my godmother. Practically family.'

Although she didn't say it, he could guess the rest. Her godmother had been more of a mother to her than her real mother.

His heart bled for her. He couldn't imagine an up-bringing where everything he did was a cause for criticism. He'd grown up knowing he was loved and valued for himself—something that Lydia had clearly never known.

On impulse, he said, 'Look, my grandparents don't live far from here. They'd be pretty upset if they found out I'd been to Trondheim and hadn't bothered to call in. I'd like to see them tomorrow evening—why don't you come with me?'

When she said nothing, he added, 'My grand-mother makes the best waffles in the entire world.'

'I…' Her eyes glittered for a moment. Longing? he wondered.

Then she swallowed. 'It's really kind of you to offer, but it's not fair of me to intrude on your family time.'

Intrude?

That word was what made him realise. Anyone Lydia had taken home had been treated by her parents as an intrusion. A nuisance. And that was how she thought of herself.

'You won't be intruding, *min kjære.* You'll be welcomed with open arms,' Jake said gently. 'Come with me.'

'You'd better check with them first.'

He knew there was no need to check, from his family's point of view, but he also realised that Lydia needed the reassurance of a proper invitation. 'I'll leave you to enjoy the window for a minute while I ring her.' He gestured towards the ceiling. 'This isn't the place to make phone calls.'

As he'd expected, his grandmother was delighted to learn that he was in Trondheim with a colleague. Before he'd even had a chance to ask if Lydia could come with him, she told him to bring his colleague for lunch.

'Thank you. We'll be there.'

'Jake, *elskling*, it will be so nice to see you.'

'And you. I've missed you,' he said, meaning it. The months he'd spent keeping everyone at a distance…what a fool he'd been. He was happiest when those he loved were close to him.

He'd be happier still if Lydia would let him close to her. But how could he be that selfish and ask that of her, when he couldn't offer her any guarantees about his future?

All the same, he slid his arms round her, holding her back against his body and nuzzling the sensitive spot behind her ear. 'My grandmother says she'd like us both to join her for lunch tomorrow. Well, actually, I didn't get the chance to ask her. She asked me first.' Just so Lydia knew she was welcome, and not an afterthought. 'Do you mind very much?'

'No, it'll be lovely. It's very kind of her. Um, is it all right to take her some flowers?'

'She'd love that. We'll find some in the morning,' he said. 'Come on. Let's do some more exploring.'

CHAPTER TEN

THE following morning, Jake picked up a hire car—complete with snow chains round the tyres—and drove them out of the city.

'Is classical music OK with you?' he asked.

'It's fine.' The notes of the piano were pure, clear and fluid, and Lydia didn't have a clue what it was. 'This is gorgeous. What is it?'

'The first movement of Bach's French Suite number five. It's perfect for driving in snow—regular and calming, and it feels like snowflakes drifting quietly down.'

She could see exactly what he meant. The music was the perfect accompaniment to the scenery outside her window. 'So what would you listen to in summer?' she asked, suddenly curious.

'If it's sunny, probably an indie band. The kind of stuff I listened to when I was a student.' He gave her an impish grin. 'You know how it is. Guys never quite grow up.'

She laughed back, but she felt her stomach tying

up in knots as they drew nearer to his grandparents' house. And when he parked she felt almost sick with nerves, even though she knew she was being ridiculous. This would probably be the only time she'd ever meet the Andersens. There was nothing to worry about. They'd *invited* her.

But still she had that feeling she'd always had when she'd brought a school report home. The feeling that she'd be scrutinised and wouldn't come up to standard.

Jake took her hand and squeezed it briefly before he opened the car door. 'Stop worrying. Everything will be fine.'

How could he be so sure?

But Lydia followed him, holding the flowers she'd chosen earlier and wishing that they were better camouflage.

Two seconds after Jake rang the doorbell, she could see two enormous dogs behind the glass door, leaping up and barking.

'Don't be scared of them. They're completely soppy,' Jake reassured her.

And then the front door opened.

The woman standing there had eyes the same colour as Jake's; her hair was the kind of soft grey that told Lydia she'd once been fair.

Her face lit up the moment she saw Jake. 'Jakob!' She hugged him and kissed him soundly on both cheeks, all the time talking rapidly in Norwegian.'

Jake introduced her. 'Lydia, this is my grand-mother, Astrid.'

'Gleder meg,' Lydia said, struggling to remember the Norwegian phrase she'd learned and really hoping that she'd pronounced it properly. *Pleased to meet you.*

'And, *Farmor*, this is Lydia, my colleague.'

Colleague. The word felt like a slap in the face.

But of course he was going to introduce her to his grandparents as his colleague. What else was he going to say—Lydia's my lover for a week? Their agree-ment was private. She knew that. So it was ridiculous to feel hurt about it. And Jake had made it clear right from the start he had no intention of taking their re-lationship any further than this single week. For pity's sake, she'd said to him herself that she wasn't looking for a relationship. He'd managed to stick to the terms of their agreement. Why couldn't she?

'I'm delighted to meet you, too, Lydia,' Astrid said, shaking her hand warmly.

'And these reprobates are Fenris and Freki—named after a Norse monster wolf and Odin's wolf.' He made a fuss of them, and Lydia crouched down beside them, letting the dogs sniff her hand and then scratching the top of their heads.

'Come in, come in. You must have coffee. And cake,' Astrid said, ushering them inside.

'Vafler?' Jake asked hopefully.

'Seeing that my oldest grandson is such a cake

fiend, I made lots of different sorts,' Astrid said dryly. 'Including *vafler.* And you're going back to England tomorrow, yes?'

'Yes.'

'I'll give you some to take to your father. And I'll email him to say what I've sent,' Astrid warned, 'so don't you dare scoff it all on the flight home.'

'As if I would.' Jake pantomimed innocence, then kissed her soundly on both cheeks. 'You're a wonderful woman. Where's *Farfar*?'

'In his study, planning yet another fishing trip. Bring him through with you,' Astrid said.

'Um—these are for you,' Lydia said shyly, handing the flowers to Astrid.

She was rewarded with an exclamation in Norwegian that she couldn't follow, but the accompanying smile told her that the older woman was pleased.

'Ah, my manners,' Astrid said. 'I apologise—I should speak English. Thank you, my dear.'

'Pleasure.'

Should she offer to help Astrid make coffee? Or should she follow Jake?

Her dilemma must have shown on her face, because Jake patted her on the shoulder. 'Come and help me fish my grandfather out of the study.'

Astrid met them in the hallway with a tray, followed by the dogs, who were looking hopeful; Per kissed the tip of her nose and took the tray from her. 'I'll carry that, *elskling.*'

But as soon as they walked into the living room, Jake's smile grew super-bright. Lydia had learned, over the last few days, that it meant that he was putting a brick wall up, because the smile didn't reach his eyes. What had upset him? she wondered.

And then she saw the photographs on the mantelpiece. Children and babies: and they were newish photographs, too, so they were clearly Astrid and Per's great-grandchildren.

Alarm bells started ringing in the back of her head. Jake was close to his family. She'd overheard him talking to them on the phone, and he'd sounded affectionate—and she'd seen his smile crinkling the corners of his eyes as he talked, so she knew his affection had been genuine. He'd greeted his grandparents warmly, too. None of this quite gelled with his insistence that he didn't want children: whatever he might say, Jakob Andersen was definitely a family man.

And right at that moment, Astrid and Per were looking anxious. Lydia followed their gazes: to Jake, to the photographs, to each other again.

She knew she was probably jumping to conclusions and there might be a perfectly reasonable explanation, but her judgement was usually sound. And she had a feeling that Jake was the only one of his generation not to have children. Astrid and Per were clearly worrying that seeing the photographs would upset him, and that led Lydia to a really nasty thought.

Had Jake lied to her?

Had his engagement broken up not because he didn't want children, but *because he couldn't have them*?

And, if that was the case, why hadn't he trusted her? She'd told him her deepest, darkest secrets. Well, maybe not all of them, but more than she'd told anyone else. And that had been the deal: that they'd talk to each other. She'd had a feeling that there was something bothering him, but every time she'd tried to broach the subject he'd brushed it aside and she'd let him fob her off with an excuse, not wanting to be too pushy.

Jake hadn't trusted her enough to tell her what was really troubling him, even though she'd confided in him.

And the knowledge hurt like hell.

'Kjetil's newest?' Jake asked, deliberately walking over to the mantelpiece and picking up the photograph of the baby.

'Little Pål,' Astrid confirmed.

'Very cute. And I know Kjetil was desperate for a boy to take fishing, this time round, after two daughters who hate mud. He must be thrilled.'

There wasn't even the slightest crack in his voice, but Lydia wasn't fooled. She'd seen Jake negotiating, and she knew he was capable of playing his cards very close to his chest. Just as he was now. Pretending everything was fine, when really it wasn't.

He replaced the photograph and gave them all another of those over-bright smiles.

'So what have you been doing in Norway?' Per asked.

'Negotiating with Nils Pedersen in Oslo—we've reached a deal that suits us both, so Andersen's will be branching out into carrying passengers as well as cargo in the spring,' Jake said. 'And, as my lawyer here was due some holiday, she decided to stay in the country for a couple of days and take a look around. So I've been playing tour guide.'

'Good. It's about time you took a break,' Per said. 'I was planning to come and kidnap you in the spring and take you fishing. And I was going to make you leave your mobile phone behind—or drop it overboard.'

'Point taken, *Farfar*,' Jake said. 'Lydia's been lecturing me about working too hard and needing to take a break.'

'Good girl,' Per said, giving her an approving smile.

How ironic, Lydia thought. Jake's grandparents had only just met her, and yet they'd already shown her more warmth and appreciation than she could ever remember receiving at home.

'So how have you enjoyed Norway, Lydia?' Astrid asked.

'It's wonderful. Though I'm hoping that we'll see the Northern Lights before I go back,' Lydia said.

'They're spectacular,' Per said. 'And if you listen very hard, sometimes you can hear them. But never whistle to them. It's bad luck.'

Astrid rolled her eyes. 'That's a fairy tale, *elskling*.'

'It makes them change shape and dance to the tune. And some say it makes them come down and sweep you away. I remember my father's father telling me what he heard, when he was a boy…' Per spread his hands. 'I know. It's a story to scare children. And no, Astrid, I won't be telling it to young Marta when Kjetil brings the children over, this weekend.'

'Lydia paints,' Jake said, abruptly changing the subject. 'And she's good. You should see her sketches.'

'May we?' Per asked.

She blinked. 'Well…if you'd really like to.'

'He's not being polite,' Jake said. 'If he was being polite, he'd smile and make some ridiculous excuse, and sneak off to make flies for fishing in the fjords, next spring.'

She could see exactly what Jake was doing. Keeping the subject as far away from children as possible. Well, he'd helped her sort her head out. This was about the only thing he was going to let her do: help take the heat off him. So, although she wouldn't normally have shown her sketchbook to a stranger, she took it from her handbag and gave it to Per. He sat on the arm of Astrid's chair and they looked through it together, his hand resting on the nape of his wife's neck.

'They're very good,' Per said eventually. 'And this one of Jake…'

'We like photographs of our grandchildren,' Astrid said, gesturing to the mantelpiece and tactfully avoiding the subject of her great-grandchildren, 'but a certain person has refused to send me one since his graduation. Even though I begged.'

'You have millions of photographs, *Farmor.* You don't need another one,' Jake protested.

'Of our eldest grandson?' Astrid asked, folding her arms and giving him a pointed look.

'I could work this up into a proper picture for you,' Lydia offered. 'In pastels—that's the medium I usually work in.'

'Would you?' Astrid looked delighted. 'We would pay you for your time and the materials, of course.'

Lydia shook her head. 'No, please. It'd be my pleasure. To say thank you for your kindness in inviting me to lunch.'

'Any friend of Jakob's is always welcome here,' Per said.

'Thank you. I'll work on the picture when I get back to England, if you don't mind waiting a little while?'

'Of course.' Astrid smiled at her. 'Would you like to see the pictures we have of Jakob as a little boy?'

Jake groaned. 'Now that's unfair, *Farmor.* Not to mention embarrassing.'

'Stop complaining. I want to show Lydia my favourite pictures of you.'

Lydia didn't have to pretend to be interested in the

photographs. Jakob had been a beautiful baby and a charming toddler; even in the gawky, awkward teenage years, he'd been stunningly good-looking.

But the things that choked her were the informal pictures. Captured moments of a family. Jake settled on his mother's lap, clearly enjoying a story being read to him. Jake on a swing, shrieking with delight as his grandfather pushed him higher. Jake riding on his father's shoulders, beaming. A laden table crowded with people at Christmas, children cuddled on their parents' laps—Jake's aunts and uncles and cousins—so obviously loved.

There were no pictures of her like that. And there were very few photographs of her as a child—only the school photographs or the ones that Polly had taken.

Jake had such a warm, loving family. His grandparents were constantly glancing at each other, touching each other's hand or laying a hand on each other's shoulder as they passed. Lydia was pretty sure that Jake's parents were the same—and that this was the kind of relationship Jake would want, too, if he'd ever let his barriers down.

Though she must've been crazy to think that she could ever push through those barriers. The fact that he hadn't told her the whole truth proved that she wasn't enough for him. Just as she hadn't been enough for Robbie to stand up to her parents—and hadn't been enough for her parents, in the first place. Not for who she was. She'd only been good enough

for them as a mini-me. And, once they learned of
her decision to resign and pursue the art she loved
so much, the gulf between her and her parents
would widen even further.

How she wished she could've had a family like
the Andersens.

But she knew it wasn't going to happen. So she
smiled, enthused over the meal, insisted on
helping to clear away afterwards and pretended
that everything was just fine: she was merely
Jake's colleague.

Lydia had gone quiet on him, Jake noticed on the
way back to Trondheim.

She hadn't said a single word since they'd left his
grandparents' house.

Hell, hell, hell. He knew he'd pushed her too
hard, too fast. She was wary of families—not sur-
prising, with parents who'd seen her as a trophy
child and gave her only the faintest of praise—and
he'd shown her what a real family was like. Close
and loving and accepting.

It must have been overwhelming for her.

No wonder she'd withdrawn.

Not that he was going to embarrass her by
drawing attention to it. He was pretty sure she
needed some space, so he reached across and
squeezed her hand briefly, hoping it would give her
the message that he understood.

But she was still quiet when they returned to their hotel.

'Lydia. I'm sorry.' He put his arms round her.

She pulled away. 'What for?' Her voice sounded slightly brittle.

'Dragging you over to see my grandparents. I realise now it must have been an ordeal for you.'

'Your grandparents,' Lydia said, 'were *lovely.*'

He frowned. 'Then what's upset you?'

Her smile was even more brittle than her voice had been. 'When were you going to tell me the truth, Jake?'

'The truth?'

'That's the thing about being a lawyer and an artist. I notice the expressions on people's faces. And your grandparents were clearly worrying about you.'

He shrugged. 'That's what grandparents do.'

'They were fine until you picked up that baby photo on the mantelpiece.'

He felt a muscle tighten in his jaw. 'I'm not with you.'

'Don't treat me like a child who needs to be humoured.' Though there was no anger in her voice. Only deep, deep hurt. 'I work things out, Jake. I read between the lines. It's what I do as a lawyer. And I know there's something you haven't told me. Something big. It's obviously to do with children—you said you didn't want kids, but I get the feeling that isn't strictly true.' She wrapped her arms round herself. 'I told you things I haven't told anyone else, even the people closest to me. I trusted you, Jake. But you…' She shook her head. 'You didn't feel you could trust me.'

'It's not that.'

'No?'

Her eyes were huge. Like a stray dog who'd been shooed away one time too many, and guilt flooded through him. He could understand why she felt betrayed. But he really hadn't meant it to be like this. 'It's really *not* that, Lydia. Of course I know I can trust you. It's just…' He sighed. 'My problem isn't fixable, and I didn't want to dump it on you.'

'But it was OK for me to dump my worries on you?'

'This week was meant to be fun. A week out of frame.'

'"Be yourself," you said. But you weren't yourself with me, were you? You held back.'

'Yes. I held back,' he admitted.

'Why?'

'I've already told you. It's not fixable.'

'Remember what you said to me about talking over a problem—how speaking it aloud makes it smaller, easier to deal with?'

He shrugged. 'I'm fine.'

'You're not, Jake. You're running from something. That's why you have huge shadows under your eyes and you work punishing hours—so you're too tired to think about whatever it is that's bothering you.'

She was right on the money. 'It's a way of dealing with it,' he said quietly.

'Carry on like this, Jake,' she warned, 'and you're going to make yourself ill.'

He couldn't help a bitter smile. 'Right.'

Her eyes narrowed as she picked up his tone. 'You're ill now? Is that what all this is about?'

He turned away, unable to look at her. Unable to face the pity he knew he'd see in her eyes. 'No.'

And then she wrapped her arms round him. Held him close.

His fingers tightened round hers; he intended to remove himself from her arms and put some distance between them. But, God help him, he couldn't do it. Not when her fingers laced between his. Not when she rested her cheek against his back.

'Remember our deal? No judgements,' she said.

His jaw clenched. 'Don't pity me. Don't you bloody *dare* pity me.'

'I'm not pitying you.'

And she also wasn't letting go of him. Wasn't turning away. She just kept holding him.

Jake resisted for as long as he could. But it felt as if something inside him had cracked and, eventually, he turned round in Lydia's arms. Closed his eyes and buried his face in the curve between her shoulder

and her neck, breathing in the scent of gardenias—
a scent he'd always associate with her, now.

Strange how the softness of her skin made him
feel stronger. And then, at last, he lifted his head.
Looked her straight in the eye.

What he saw wasn't pity. Concern, yes; but no pity.

And, finally, he was able to get the words out.

CHAPTER ELEVEN

'THAT sabbatical I had, eighteen months ago… It wasn't a sabbatical.'

Once Jake taken that first step and started talking, it was surprisingly easy to carry on. Because Lydia still had her arms round him, letting him know that she was there and she wasn't going anywhere.

'I found a lump. I knew I ought to go and do something about it, but I kept putting it off. I was busy stepping into Dad's shoes, and I thought it was probably a cyst.' He'd brushed it aside. Buried his head in the sand. 'I thought it could wait.'

She said nothing, but she held him just a little bit more tightly.

'It turned out that it couldn't. And I wish to hell I'd gone to see my doctor earlier.'

'Cancer?' she asked gently.

He nodded. God, how he hated that word. The way it had blown his life apart and left gaping craters in place of his dreams.

'What were you—twenty-nine?'

'Twenty-eight. I'd never smoked, I ate sensibly, and I didn't drink too much. I exercised, I managed my stress levels. I thought I was doing all the right things. I never dreamed I could…' He blew out a breath. 'One minute, I was seeing my GP for what I thought was something minor. The next, I was at the hospital, waiting for a scan. I was still expecting them to tell me it was just a cyst and give me some tablets to make it go away. But I knew before the consultant said a word that it was bad news.' He gave a mirthless laugh. 'Testicular cancer. I was too shocked to take it in, at first. But then I was full of questions. I wanted to know what my options were, what I could expect from the future.'

And the answers had been tough to face.

Tougher still for Grace. She hadn't been able to deal with it. At all.

'I had surgery,' he said slowly. 'But it had spread a bit. So I had radiotherapy as well. To nuke the thing from my body.'

'Did it work?'

'The consultant was pleased at my last check-up. I'm up to a year between appointments, now. But it's…' He sighed. 'It's changed things for me. Thanks to the radiotherapy, let's just say we didn't actually need to use a condom this week.'

She kissed him swiftly on the mouth. 'I promised you I wouldn't pity you. And I don't. But I hope you'll at least let me sympathise. It's rough, having your options taken away from you—especially at your age. I take it your family knows the whole story?'

'Yes. It's why my grandparents were a bit…uncomfortable about my seeing the photographs. I'm the only one of my generation without kids, and they think it upsets me.'

'Does it?'

He wasn't ready to answer that one. 'I'm fine with my career. I love my job.' He smiled wryly. 'Though my mother nags me about working too hard. She worries I'll give myself a relapse.'

'But if you let up the pace, you'd have time to think and brood and dwell on your regrets. What might have been.'

He looked at her. 'It's the same for you, isn't it?'

'It was, once. Except I've come to my decision. I know what I want to do. What I'm going to do.' She stroked his face. 'What about you?'

'I'm fine. I've come to terms with it—really, I have. I've had eighteen months to get used to the idea.'

'Really?'

'Really.'

'You've got your barriers up again,' she said. 'Because your smile doesn't reach your eyes.'

'I'm fine,' he repeated. Say it often enough, and he'd start to believe his own lies.

'This week was meant to be bouncing ideas off each other.'

'We have,' he said.

'I've given you *nothing*, Jake.'

'This week was also meant to be about hot sex. You've given me that,' he pointed out with a grin.

'But I haven't helped you move forward, the way you helped me.'

'You've given me time out of frame,' he said. 'That's helped me more than you could ever guess.'

'Time out of frame.' She stared at him. 'And that's it?'

'That's it. Tomorrow, we go back to England. You start your new life, and I go back to running Andersen Marine.' He stole a kiss. 'Lydia, I've done enough talking for now. Can we go back to the hot sex bit now, please?'

That was what this whole week had been about, for him.

Hot sex.

And he'd just made it pretty clear that he didn't want anything more from her. Even though he'd talked to her, told her something he clearly hadn't shared with anyone outside his immediate family, he clearly wasn't prepared to make anything more of what was happening between them—or even discuss it.

I've done enough talking for now.

And that hurt. Hurt like hell that he wasn't prepared to consider any other future. To talk over the idea that maybe there was room for him in her new life, and room for her in his.

Yet again, she hadn't measured up. Wasn't enough to change his mind.

But tonight was their last night. A very private goodbye. She wasn't going to ruin it by brooding. She was going to make the best of it: take what he'd give her, and try not to break her heart over the fact that she wanted more.

She stood on tiptoe, reached up and touched her lips to his.

His eyes darkened; he walked over to the window to close the curtains, still not relinquishing her hand, and switched on the bedside lamp. And then tenderly, so sweetly that it almost broke her heart, he slid his fingers into her hair, cupping her jaw with his palms. She could see him looking at her mouth, then back to her eyes, then back to her mouth again, and slowly, slowly, he leaned towards her. Her lips had already parted and he caught her lower lip between his, the pressure telling her how much he wanted her, yet gentle and tender at the same time.

It made her want to cry.

He helped her shrug out of her sweater, and then he allowed her to do the same for him. Item for item. Equal. Until they were both skin to skin, lying on the bed with their bodies tangled together. She stroked his skin as if her fingertips could store every curve, every plane, every angle of his body in her memory. Breathed in his scent. Brushed tiny, nibbling kisses over his body.

And he was doing the same, touching and kissing and nuzzling and stroking until she was quivering with sheer need.

Lydia didn't trust her voice not to crack, betray her feelings, so she kept the words back. But they echoed in her head: *I love you. Except you're not going to let me. So this is goodbye.*

He moved to kneel between her thighs.

'Jake.' She reached out to touch his face. 'No.'

'You'd rather we didn't?'

'It's not that.' She shook her head. 'Just…' How could she put this without sounding completely wanton? Then again, she had nothing left to lose, so she might as well say it. 'Neither of us sleeps around. In the circumstances, we don't need a condom.' She drew the pad of her thumb along his lower lip. 'I don't want any barriers between us.'

'Are you sure about that?' he checked.

'Absolutely sure,' she whispered. 'No condom. Just you and me. Skin to skin.'

'Lydia Sheridan, you're one hell of a woman,' he said, and kissed her. And behind the heat there was a sweetness and tenderness, a weird sensation she couldn't name but she knew she'd never felt before.

Slowly, gently, he eased his body into hers.

She closed her eyes tightly, willing the tears to stay back.

They'd had an agreement.

And she was going to stick to it, even though it hurt like hell.

She slid her hands into his hair and wrapped her legs round his thighs, drawing him deeper and jamming her mouth against his. This was it. The beginning of their last night together. The last time she'd feel him inside her. The last time he'd touch her, hold her, call her *elskling* or *min kjære*.

And as her climax hit she couldn't stop the single tear leaking down her cheek.

To her relief, Jake didn't notice; he simply curled his body round hers afterwards and drew her back against him. She lay awake for a long, long time, listening to his regular breathing, before she finally drifted into sleep. And her eyes felt gritty, the next morning, when the alarm shrilled to wake them.

Jake rolled over to switch off the alarm, then rolled back to glance at Lydia. She looked like hell, and he felt incredibly guilty. He hadn't exactly been fair to her. But what else could he have done?

It would be, oh, so easy to say, 'I've changed my mind about our agreement. I don't want it to be just a week. I want more. I want everything you can give me.' It wasn't as if his words would come completely out of the blue. He'd given her a big enough hint—he'd taken her to meet his family. A woman as clever and perceptive as Lydia would surely have picked up the fact that he didn't take just anyone home.

Funny. In business he would've cut to the chase, got the problem out into the open and worked out a compromise to suit everyone.

But this was personal. Which was a whole different ball game.

And it wasn't solely his feelings that he had to consider. Lydia had admitted that she wanted children of her own. She'd been great with Nils's children. And he'd seen the look in her eyes, the softness in her face, when his grandmother had shown her those pictures of him as a baby. Lydia would make a great mother, one day. He couldn't take that option away from her.

Besides, there were no guarantees he'd stay in remission.

And she was starting a new life. Doing what she really wanted to do. He had nothing to offer her except burdens, in the future. How could he be selfish enough to take comfort from her, while knowing that she would be left to pick up the pieces on her own?

So he wasn't going to ask her. He'd do the right thing, just as he had with Grace. He'd let her go, and hope that she found someone who deserved her.

He just wished it could've been him.

Though now wasn't the time to wallow in misery. He was going to be brisk and bright and cheery.

Pretend this was a business deal. He'd make it as painless as he could for both of them.

'We'd better get up now, if we want breakfast before we leave.'

'I'm not particularly hungry.'

Neither was he, but he'd learned to mask his feelings over the last few months. Exactly as he was doing right now. 'Do you want the first shower, or shall I?' He didn't dare suggest that they showered together. Because last night had been goodbye, and if he made love with her again, he might not be able to let her go.

'It doesn't have to be this way, Jake.'

'How do you mean?' he asked.

'It doesn't have to be time out of frame.' Her eyes were dark and beseeching. 'We could make this work.'

He shook his head. 'You know why we can't.'

'Look at it from a different perspective, Jake. The chances are, you'll stay in remission and you'll be around for years. But if things don't pan out that way, wouldn't it be better to…' she stumbled slightly over the word '…to die knowing that you've given people precious memories to keep, so they can remember you with smiles? Sure, the people in your life will miss you like hell when you've gone and they'll grieve for you, but there'll come a time when they can remember you with smiles. And at least they'll have those memories to sustain them, instead of regrets that they didn't try harder to break down your walls.'

It would be so easy to believe it. He wanted so badly to believe it.

But it was easy to say and a hell of a lot less easy to live it.

He'd seen what it did to Grace. How it had changed her from an outgoing woman into a mess.

And Lydia was fragile to start with. She'd spent years being a perfectionist, trying to be the best she could be and please other people. Could he really expect her to handle this burden, too? For her sake, he had to say no. 'I think,' he said, 'that I prefer you when you're being an artist. When you're sketching and you don't talk.'

'So you're not even going to consider it?'

'I'm asking you to trust my judgement on this, Lydia.'

'Why can't you trust my judgement, instead?'

'Because,' he said quietly, 'there's too much at stake.' He owed it to her to be honest, at least. 'Yes, we could have a relationship. And you're the only woman who's come anywhere near tempting me to it. But it's not going to happen.' He dragged in a breath. 'Every day I'll grow to hate the face I see in the mirror, knowing that I'm taking your options away. I can't give you children and I can't give you a future. And that's not fair.'

She propped herself on her elbow and looked him straight in the eye. 'There are ways round it if we want to have children. Adoption, fostering and IVF, to name three of them. I'm not saying it'd be easy, but surely you can see that there are possibilities? That your way isn't the only way?'

'No. It's not negotiable, Lydia.'

'You're impossible! Why do you have to be so stubborn about this, Jake?'

Did she really not know? 'Because, if the positions were reversed, losing you would be like losing half myself. And I'm not prepared to put you through that.'

'Doing it your way, I don't even get you at all.'

And it was better that way. It would be less painful, in the long run. 'We agreed: this was a week out of frame.'

'Supposing I want more than a week, Jake?'

'Supposing I don't?' He knew he was lying, even as he said it. And when he saw her flinch, he hated himself for hurting her. But he had to be cruel to be kind. He had to do the right thing.

'I guess that says it all. You'd better have the first shower, while I pack my stuff.' She turned her face away from him, and he knew there were tears in her eyes. Tears she was trying to hide from him. Tears he'd caused.

But he knew this was the best way. They'd had a week together. A week in which he'd fallen for her, just as she'd fallen for him. But in a single week…neither of them had fallen too deeply in love. Yes, it hurt to end things now, but at least they both had a chance of getting over it—and Lydia had the chance of finding happiness. Whereas if he let himself be selfish and did things her way, if he spent whatever time he had left with her—every day, they'd fall a little further, a little deeper. And that would make the end devastatingly painful.

This was the best way.

It *was*.

The journey back to London was the worst Lydia had ever experienced. The travelling went smoothly enough—both flights were on time and there were no problems with their connections. But Jake had his over-bright smile in place and he was clearly in businessman mode, making sure that his feelings were masked from her. And he kept every single topic of conversation strictly neutral.

Nothing she could do, nothing she could say, would be enough to change his mind where their situation was concerned.

It's not negotiable.

She couldn't even take refuge in sketching, because when she did make the effort, the pictures came out all wrong. Sheer frustration blocked her creative instincts. Part of her still wanted to rail at him, to yell at him that he was being stubborn and difficult and impossibly proud, and he ought to be man enough to admit that she was right, but she knew that the middle of a crowded flight really wasn't the place to have a row. And it wasn't the sort of conversation she could conduct in a whisper.

By the time they reached London, her temper was near boiling point, and she was as angry with herself as she was with Jake. She'd promised herself that, after Robbie, she'd never put herself in another position where someone could break her heart.

And what had she done? Fallen head over heels for someone else who'd rejected her. Stupid, stupid, stupid.

Well, there was one thing she could do. She could refuse to let him see just how hurt and angry she was. Play it uber-cool. So, even though she wanted to yell and scream and throw the most enormous tantrum in history, she pinned a smile to her face as she followed him through Customs and pretended that everything was absolutely fine. She collected her luggage and walked with him to the doorway of the airport.

'So, it's the end of our week,' she said brightly. 'Back to London; back to normal.'

'Yes.' He looked wary; no doubt he was worrying that she was going to make some big dramatic scene. Well, she wasn't. 'Thank you for showing me round in Norway,' she said politely.

'Pleasure. Though I'm sorry you didn't get to see the Northern Lights.'

'You couldn't help the weather.' She shrugged. 'Well, I'd better be going. I have things to do.'

Nothing that important. Nothing she wouldn't have dropped for him. But he was too proud to ask her, and she knew he'd throw it back in her face if she offered. And she had no intention of letting him reject her again; she had her pride, too. 'I'll have that letter ready for you on Monday morning.'

'Letter?'

'My resignation letter,' she reminded him. 'Backdated to the beginning of last week. Which leaves me two weeks' notice to work, less remaining annual leave and time in lieu.' She'd worked it out on the plane. 'Which gives me eight working days. I'll be leaving Andersen's a week on Wednesday.'

For a moment, he looked shocked. Upset, even. Did that mean that he wasn't going to let her walk out of his life, after all?

But then he masked his expression. 'I'm sure Human Resources can work out something to your mutual satisfaction. If not, refer them to me and I'll sort it.'

And his words taught her that there was still a corner of her heart left to break, a tiny bit of hope left to be squashed.

He was going to let her walk away.

And there wasn't a thing she could do about it.

Only her pride kept her back straight and her face expressionless. 'Thank you.' She held out her hand to shake his. 'Goodbye, Jake.'

He took her hand. Shook it briefly.

And she made sure that she was the first to turn away.

CHAPTER TWELVE

ON MONDAY morning, Lydia walked into the office, quietly left an envelope with Jake's PA, and spent a wary day at her desk.

Please, don't let her have to face Jake. Let him be busy with other parts of his empire. And don't let him have changed his mind over the weekend and make her stay at Andersen's for a single minute more than necessary.

She wasn't sure whether she was more relieved or disappointed that her prayers were answered and she didn't even hear Jake's name mentioned during the day. Matt tried to persuade her to change her mind about resigning, but she stood firm on the issue. Even if she hadn't already decided to follow her heart and try to make her living from painting, there was no way she could continue working at Andersen's. Not after what had happened between her and Jake. It was way, way too awkward.

Though her phone beeped that evening with a message from him.

She glanced at the text. *You OK?*

No, she wasn't. She was as miserable as hell. But Jake Andersen was the last person she'd admit it to. Anyway, he wasn't asking her personally. He was obviously doing the concerned boss bit, checking that Human Resources had done what she asked. So she'd answer him accordingly. *Fine, thanks. HR were very good*, she texted back.

She almost—almost—asked how he was. But she knew he'd say he was fine, whether he was or not, so it was pointless asking.

Jake wasn't in the office for the next couple of days; Lydia was careful not to ask, but learned that he was away on business—well, if you took a week off unscheduled, of course you'd have a lot of ground to make up. And she had plenty to occupy herself with: tying up loose ends at Andersen's, and making contact with gallery owners and craft shops and website designers.

Not to mention doing the picture she'd promised to his grandparents.

She tackled that first. Even though every stroke of her pencil made her miss him even more.

Jake worked in his hotel room on Wednesday night until the figures on the spreadsheet in front of him were blurred.

And then he sat back and brooded.

It was meant to be easier, being out of the office—

so there was no chance he'd accidentally bump into Lydia in a corridor, or catch a glimpse of her in a meeting room, or hear her voice.

Except not seeing her was worse.

Was she right? Was he being difficult and stupidly stubborn by trying to let her go and give her the chance of future happiness with someone else? Would it be better to grieve with memories, than to grieve with regrets?

Jake thought about it for a long, long time. In the end, he picked up his mobile phone to call her. But he glanced at the clock and realised that it was two in the morning: perhaps not the most reasonable time to call someone.

Instead, he sent her a text. *Lydia, you were right and I was wrong. I'm sorry. We need to talk. Have dinner with me on Friday?*

He just hoped that she wouldn't be as stubborn about it as he'd been.

The next morning, during the break in his meeting, he rang a jewellery designer he knew, with a very specific request. Something to show Lydia that he really meant what he said.

He checked his phone subtly every half hour for the rest of the day, expecting to see her reply.

But nothing. Not even a refusal. *Nothing.*

Odd.

Unless she was so angry with him that she didn't trust herself to reply. A text message probably wasn't the best way to handle it, and flowers, sent to the office, would only embarrass her. No, he'd have to be patient. He'd wait until he was back in London—and then he'd discuss it with her face to face. He'd make up some excuse for a meeting, if he had to.

Except, when he was back in London on Friday, Lydia wasn't. Matt had sent her down to the south coast to deal with something.

Oh, for pity's sake.

If he were the paranoid type, he'd think that everything was conspiring against him.

OK. He'd go and see her on Saturday at her flat. Armed with flowers and an apology.

But in the middle of the morning he got a phone call from his mother that made him drop everything and catch the next flight to Trondheim.

'You're miserable,' Polly said, folding her arms and looking sternly at her god-daughter. 'Talk to me.'

Lydia shrugged it off. 'I'm fine.'

'No, you're not. I've been talking to Em, and she thinks the same. Something's wrong.'

'I'm fine,' Lydia fibbed again. 'Just busy, sorting out work. And thank you for persuading Natasha to give me a chance at the gallery.'

'Natasha Romanov might dress like a ditzy chick,' Polly said, 'but she's the most hard-headed businesswoman I've ever met. She's exhibiting your work purely because she thinks you're going to go far and she's going to make a serious killing when your prices start rising. Which they will, because—apart from the fact that you're good—the smart money nowadays is going into fine art rather than company shares.'

'Thank you. I think,' Lydia said, topping up her godmother's coffee.

'Have you spoken to your parents?'

'Since Dad's hissy fit? No.' Lydia shrugged. 'Still, at least it's out in the open now. And this time I'm not going crawling back, looking for their approval. I've made the right choice for me. And if they can't come to terms with it, it's their problem. I can't help being female.'

Polly blinked. 'What does being female have to do with it, Lyddie?'

'You know as well as I do, I was a mistake—and Dad wanted a son. I've been a disappointment to him right from the start.' Lydia shrugged again. 'Don't worry about it. I've lived with it for years. Except now it's finally stopped hurting.' She looked her godmother straight in the eye. 'I've spent years trying to be something I'm not, to please them, and it hasn't worked. So now we're going to do this on my terms. This is who I am, Polly. He's going to have to accept me for who I am. And so is my mother.'

'You think your parents wanted a son?' Polly bit her lip. 'I *told* Ruth she ought to be honest with you.'

'Honest with me about what?'

Polly shook her head. 'I can't break a confidence. It's not my place to tell you. You need to talk to her.'

'She's not even speaking to me right now,' Lydia pointed out.

Polly looked awkward. 'I know, love. You're going to have to make the first move.'

'I'm not sure I want to.'

'Lyddie, trust me, this is a conversation you really need to have—before you can really move on. Tell her you need to talk to her about something confidential. Then, when you see her, tell her what you just told me.'

'And that's really going to make a difference?'

Polly sighed. 'If she doesn't tell you, ask her about Daniel.'

Lydia frowned. 'Who's Daniel?'

'I've already said enough.' Polly hugged her. 'Too much, probably. But right now you're bone-deep miserable—and it's my place, as your godmother, to help you do something about it.'

'I'm fine. I'm finally going to be doing what I love.'

'That's not what I'm talking about, Lyddie, and you know it,' Polly said quietly. 'There's someone, isn't there?'

'What makes you think that?'

'Because I've seen this look on your face before. After Robbie.'

'I'm fine.'

Polly took her hands. 'No, you're not. It's the guy you keep sketching, isn't it?'

Lydia felt her eyes widen. 'You looked in my sketchbook?'

'No. I did think about it,' Polly admitted, 'because I know you retreat into drawing rather than tackling things head-on, but I wouldn't invade your privacy like that. No—you have a habit of doodling when you're talking. You left a picture on my kitchen memo-pad, last week. He's beautiful.'

'I don't want to talk about it.'

'Not talking about things,' Polly said gently, drawing her into a hug, 'has caused your mother a lot of heartache. Don't make the same mistake.'

'We agreed, it was a single week.'

'Your week in Norway?' Polly asked.

Lydia bit her lip and nodded.

'I wondered why you sounded so happy, in your texts. You had this zest for life I hadn't seen in you since you were sixteen.'

'It was one single week,' Lydia reiterated. 'The idea was, we'd have some space to think and get it out of our systems.'

'But it didn't get him out of yours.'

Lydia swallowed miserably. 'No.'

'So what's to say it got you out of his?'

'It did. I'm sure.'

'I think you need to talk to him. Be honest. Because what have you got to lose, Lyddie?'

Lydia sucked in a breath. 'Everything.'

'Wrong, love. You've got everything to play for.'

Polly paused. 'You know I borrowed that book of postcards from you, last week? There was a portrait on your desk, and I'm afraid I couldn't help seeing it. It's the best picture you've ever done.'

Lydia shrugged off the compliment. 'I promised his grandparents I'd do them a picture.'

'His grandparents?' Polly blinked. 'You met them?'

'We were staying nearby. He could hardly have refused to see them.'

'But he took you to meet them.'

'As his colleague.'

'For such a bright woman, you can be incredibly dense. What was he going to say? "Here's a woman I'm having a fling with"?' Polly stroked Lydia's hair back from her forehead. 'Is he close to his family?'

'Yes.'

'He wouldn't take you to meet them unless he thought you were special—because they'd grill him about you.'

Lydia's frown deepened. 'My parents have never grilled me.'

'Because your parents,' Polly said, 'are emotionally straitjacketed. Normal families grill you about things. Just like Em and I do.'

That much was true. And hadn't she said to Jake that she was closer to her godmother and her best friend than she was to her parents?

'When did you send that picture to his grandparents?' Polly asked.

'The framer in Trondheim promised to deliver it to them by the end of this week.'

'The second they see it,' Polly assured her, 'they'll be on the phone to him. And he'll call you.'

'What if he doesn't?'

'Given that men can also be stupid, stubborn, blinkered and too proud... Then you'll have to call him.' Polly patted her shoulder. 'And, just so you know, Em and I will nag you until you do.'

'*Farmor*, you can't spend the night sitting in a chair at *Farfar*'s bedside,' Jake said.

'But if anything happens—'

'The hospital will ring my mobile phone,' he cut in gently, 'and I'll drive you straight here. We're fifteen minutes away, that's all. You'll be much more comfortable at home, you'll get some rest, and *Farfar* won't be worrying himself sick about you. And isn't it best to take the worries off his shoulders?'

'I know you're right, Jakob.' Astrid let him enfold her in his arms for a moment. 'He has to pull through this. I can't imagine life without Per.'

'Of course he'll pull through,' Jake reassured her. 'He'll be back fishing in the spring and leaving bits of boat engine in the kitchen, the way he always does, driving you crazy.'

Once Jake had settled his grandmother at home, he telephoned round the family to give them an update on Per.

And then he sat and brooded. There was no way he'd be back in England for at least the next week: which meant he'd miss Lydia's leaving do. He could call her and explain—but then again, what he wanted to say to her was something that needed to be said face to face. He couldn't let his family down; but equally he didn't want to let her down. Whatever he did, someone was going to get hurt.

Right now, his grandmother needed him more; if Lydia gave him the chance to explain, he was pretty sure she'd see it the same way.

In the end, he emailed Ingrid, his PA.

I'm going to be in Norway until my grandfather's home, so I won't make Lydia's leaving do. Can you ask Matt to do the speech for me? And I've missed the collection for her present, so can you put something in for me? Make sure that there's enough for a decent-sized box of pastels, even if you have to double the funds, and I'll settle up with you when I'm back. Thanks, J.

Jake and Astrid visited his grandfather every day; Jake made sure that his grandmother ate properly, and when his cousins came to visit he ended up entertaining their children with the stories he remembered Per telling him when he was a child.

Ironic. He'd spent the last eighteen months avoiding children. And now here he was, Uncle Jakob who told stories with silly voices and sang songs and let the kids climb all over him—just as he'd once done with his own uncles, as a child. And just as he'd once thought he'd do with his own children.

On the Thursday night, when they got back from the hospital, a neighbour dropped round with a parcel.

'I can't remember ordering anything. Maybe it's a Christmas present.'

Jake looked at the return address. 'It's from a picture-framer in Trondheim.'

'Picture-framer?' Astrid wrinkled her nose. 'I know I'm leaning on you, *elskling*, but would you…?'

'Of course. And you're not leaning on me. That's what grandsons are for,' Jake told her firmly.

But he was truly surprised when he opened the parcel. It contained a portrait of him, mounted properly and framed.

He knew that Lydia had promised his grandparents a portrait, but he hadn't expected her to go through with it. Or to have it professionally framed and couriered to them.

But what really caught his attention was the pose.

He definitely hadn't posed for this picture. It was almost a side-on view; he was gazing out into the distance with a wistful, dreamy look on his face and his lips slightly parted. And the tender light in his eyes…

This was a picture of a man in love.

And it could only have been painted by someone

who could see into his heart. By someone who felt that same wistful yearning.

By someone who loved him.

So maybe, just maybe, there was a chance.

'Jake?'

He showed his grandmother the portrait.

'It's beautiful.' Her eyes filled with tears. 'Per will be so pleased.'

'Well, it's another reason for him to come home quickly.'

'You will thank her for me, give her my love?'

'In person,' Jake promised. The minute he was back in England, he'd go and see Lydia.

And hope that she'd let him through her barriers.

On Friday morning, Lydia knocked on the door of her mother's office and walked in.

'Oh, so you've come to your senses?' Ruth asked, looking approvingly at Lydia's business suit. 'Good. And I'd be pleased to help you with some contacts, as you're looking for a new job.'

'I'm not looking for a job.' Lydia tried to damp down her impatience. 'I'm only wearing this because I thought you might prefer it to jeans with streaks of pastels down them. As I said on the phone, we need to talk.'

'About what?' Ruth asked.

Lydia took a deep breath. 'I know you disapprove of my decision to change career, but I've spent most of my life trying to be a dutiful daughter, and it just hasn't worked. So now I'm doing what I want to do. I know you can't forgive me for not being Daniel, but—'

'*What* did you just say?' Ruth demanded, her face white.

Lydia frowned. 'You can't forgive me for not being Daniel.'

'How do you know about Daniel?' Ruth's eyes narrowed.

'I don't, not really.'

Ruth's eyes narrowed. 'Has Polly been talking to you about him?'

Oh, no. She wasn't going to drop her godmother in it. 'I worked it out for myself. It's pretty obvious: I wasn't your only child. I don't know whether you miscarried or Daniel died as a baby, or whether he was older or younger than me, but I realise that you and Dad have spent most of my life wishing that my brother hadn't died.' She tried hard not to let her voice shake with the pain lancing through her. This had to come out, or it would fester. 'That it had been me, instead.'

Ruth closed her eyes and sat down behind her desk again. 'Lydia, no. It's not that. Not at all.' Lines of strain showed on her face. 'Daniel wasn't your brother.'

Lydia frowned. 'Then who was he?'

'Daniel... He was your father,' Ruth said heavily.

'My *father*? What?' Lydia stared at her mother. 'No. My birth certificate has all the right dates. Dad's details are all there on it.'

'Because he agreed to let me fill them in. Edward Sheridan isn't your biological father,' Ruth elaborated.

She had to be in some kind of parallel universe. 'You were married before?' But she had no memories of anyone called Daniel. No memories of any other family. 'I thought you and—' She hesitated over the word 'Dad'. 'I thought you'd been married for years before I came along.'

'We were.'

'Then how…?' She thought fast. 'I'm adopted?'

'No.' Ruth bit her lip. 'It isn't a pretty story, and I'm not proud of myself.'

It was an admission that Lydia had never, ever expected to hear. And she was still too stunned by the news that her father wasn't her father to speak.

Eventually, Ruth filled the silence. 'I fell in love with Daniel when I was a student, years before I met your father. We were planning to get married—but then he went to Paris for six months, to study. He…met someone else.'

Lydia could see from her mother's expression that the memories still hurt. She must have loved Daniel very, very much.

'And then I met your—' She stopped. 'I met Edward.'

Clearly on the rebound. Had Edward realised?

'We wanted the same things out of life, so we decided to get married.'

What about love? Or had Ruth not been able to love anyone since Daniel? Lydia had so many questions, she barely knew where to start asking. But she also knew that now wasn't the right time to talk. If she sidetracked her mother now, Ruth might never talk about this again—and Lydia needed to know the facts. She needed to know who she really was.

So she waited.

'It was fine at first, but then we went through a bad patch. And right about that time Daniel came back to London and I bumped into him at a party.' She dragged in a breath. 'It was as if Paris had never happened.'

'You had an affair with him?' Lydia was really shocked. This kind of thing happened to other people—not her parents. Not her straight-laced parents, with their insistence on doing everything by the rules. She could hardly believe what she was hearing.

'I didn't plan it that way.' Ruth sighed heavily. 'I was going to leave Edward, set up home with Daniel. But then he was killed in a car crash.'

The bleakness on Ruth's face told Lydia just how much her mother had loved Daniel. That she still missed him. Still found herself thinking of him.

'And then, a month after the funeral, I discovered I was expecting you.'

The child of Ruth's dead lover. No wonder her parents had both pushed her away. She was a visible reminder of her mother's betrayal, and neither of her parents had ever been able to deal with it.

'You're absolutely definite that I'm not…that I'm Daniel's child?'

'You look like him.' Ruth bit her lip. 'And Edward had mumps as a child.'

As the ramifications sank in Lydia felt sick.

Her father couldn't have children.

Just like Jake.

So it wasn't just that Lydia was living proof of her mother's betrayal; every time Edward looked at her, he saw what he hadn't been able to give his wife. And feeling like a failure wasn't something that would sit well with a man like Edward Sheridan, a man who'd been such a success in his career. No wonder he'd always been so hard on her and moved the goalposts so frequently. In an odd way, he hadn't wanted her to be able to live up to his expectations: because she wasn't his child.

'Edward and I talked about the situation and he agreed to raise you as his.'

Lydia couldn't even begin to imagine how that conversation had gone. Or understand why Edward had agreed to it. Had he loved Ruth that much? Yet she could never remember physical affection between her parents. Not like the warmth she'd seen between Jake's grandparents.

'But he never really saw me as his daughter,' Lydia said. 'He saw me as Daniel's child.'

Ruth didn't answer, and Lydia felt sick. Her mother's silence indicated that Lydia's assessment was accurate.

'You said you'd left Edward. Didn't you think about…?' She couldn't ask that. Couldn't bear to consider the idea that her mother had thought about terminating her pregnancy. 'About bringing me up on your own?' she asked finally.

'My parents were too old to help me. Polly would've stood by me, but I couldn't burden her like that.'

Ha. There was an irony. Polly was about the one person in Lydia's life who didn't see her as a burden.

'Why didn't you let Daniel's family bring me up?' Surely they would have wanted their son's baby?

'Edward and I agreed to raise you as his child.'

To save face? Lydia's lip curled. 'So I've got another family out there. People who might have loved me for who I am.'

'They don't know about you.'

And Lydia noted the part that her mother didn't deny. 'Maybe you should have told them.'

'It wouldn't have made any difference.'

'No? Every time you see me, you feel guilt and Dad—' well, what else could she call him? '—feels resentment.'

'You're being rather melodramatic, Lydia.' Ruth's

tone alerted Lydia to that fact that her mother was back to being the cool, unemotional woman Lydia knew: in charge of the situation and in strict control of herself.

'Melodramatic? Hardly, Mum. I've spent years feeling that I was never really loved, trying hard to make you and Dad proud of me and always failing.'

'Lyd—'

'No—I think it's time you listened to me, for once. I had a miserable childhood. I've wasted years of my life trying to please you both by following you into law, instead of doing the one thing I knew I was really good at. And now you're telling me that the man I always thought was my father is nothing of the kind. That everything I've always believed is a pack of lies. I think,' Lydia said, folding her arms, 'if I threw the biggest tantrum on earth right now, it'd be pretty understandable.'

'I didn't bring you up to have tantrums.'

'No.' Her mother hadn't brought her up at all. And how she could deliver a bombshell like this so coolly, so calmly, was beyond Lydia. 'I don't think,' she said quietly, 'there's much left to say. But perhaps you'd answer one question for me. Why were you so set against me being an artist? Does that have anything to do with Daniel?'

Ruth inclined her head. Just once. 'He was an artist.'

No details. Not that Lydia had expected them from her mother. Hopefully Polly would fill in the gaps.

But at least it told her why Edward Sheridan had been so angry about her choices. Going to art college would have been like following in Daniel's footsteps. Rubbing yet more salt in Edward's wounds.

'Thank you.' Lydia stood up. 'That was…enlightening. I'll let you get on. In the circumstances, I think you'll understand why I'd rather not have lunch with you today.'

She didn't wait for a response; she simply left.

She'd already turned her mobile phone off before she went to see her mother; she left it switched off and walked through St James' Park down to the Thames, and from there along the riverbank to the Tate Gallery. The place she'd always gone when she needed to think; she sat down in her favourite room, though she couldn't focus on a single one of the paintings.

Last time she'd gone to a gallery, it had been hand in hand with Jake.

And now…it felt as if her whole life had been shaken up, turned inside out, and left at a skewed angle. Nothing made sense any more.

She sat there until one of the staff came over and gently told her that the gallery was closing and she needed to leave.

'Sorry. I…' There weren't any words, so she just gave an apologetic smile and left.

She really didn't feel like going home. Not yet. But

Emma would just be getting home, tired from a week's teaching, and, as it was Friday, Polly was probably out. All the same, Lydia took her mobile phone from her bag to ring her godmother, just in case, and realised that the phone was still switched off. The second she turned it on, it began to beep. Texts and voicemails—every half an hour, on the dot—from her godmother. To check that she was all right.

Given the number of messages, Polly must be worried sick. She speed-dialled Polly's number.

'Lyddie? Thank God. Are you all right?'

No. 'I forgot my phone was switched off. I went to the Tate.'

'Your mother rang me.'

'Sorry. I didn't mean to drop you in it.'

'The important thing is that you're all right. Where are you?'

'Walking by the Thames—and no, I'm not going to do anything stupid. I just want to be on my own for a bit.'

'You'd be better off,' Polly said, 'over here, eating carbs and talking it through. Well, it won't take ten minutes to cook some pasta. Turn up when you're ready.'

Lydia had a feeling that if she didn't turn up, her godmother would come in search of her. So she took the Tube and headed for Polly's flat.

Polly greeted her with a hug and a large glass of red wine. 'You look shell-shocked.'

Lydia nodded. 'I feel as if I don't know who I am any more.'

'I'll tell you who you are,' Polly said. 'You're Lydia Sheridan. You draw like an angel, you're kind and you're clever and you're beautiful and I'm incredibly proud of you.'

Lydia felt the tears filling her eyes. 'Sometimes, Pol, I really wish you'd been my mother.'

'So,' Polly said fiercely, 'do I. Come and sit down in the kitchen while I cook the pasta. And don't argue. Did Ruth tell you about Daniel?'

'She told me he's my father.' And very little more than that. 'So what was he like? I mean, if he dumped her as soon as he got to Paris, he wasn't the committed sort, was he?'

'He was twenty-one—a year older than your mother and me. We all make mistakes when we're young,' Polly said. 'Actually, he was a nice guy. Good company, full of fun.'

'Would I have liked him?'

Polly nodded. 'And he would've adored you.'

They were talking about a man she'd never met, a man whose name she'd never heard before this week—and yet the fact that he would've approved of her was oddly comforting.

'What kind of artist was he?'

'Landscape. He liked working with pastels, the way you do—he liked the immediacy.'

For a moment, Lydia wondered if he'd ever

painted Ruth, the way she'd painted Jake. Then again, she couldn't imagine her mother showing any of the emotions that Jake had shown.

'He liked painting reflections. That picture over my fireplace is one of his.'

'The Tower of London reflected in the Thames? I've always liked that picture.' And she too enjoyed painting reflections. For the first time in years, Lydia could see a gap where she might have fitted into someone's life. 'Why didn't she tell Daniel's family about me?'

'I can't answer that one, love.'

Lydia sighed. 'I don't even know his full name, or where he's buried, or anything.'

'I can tell you all that,' Polly said, 'but if you're thinking about contacting his family—I don't know where they are now, or even whether his parents are still alive. And after all these years…it might be a bit of a shock for them to find out about you.'

'Better not to know?'

'No, just that Daniel's parents would be in their late seventies and, the older you get, the harder it is to adjust to things. Lydia, any family would be proud to have you as part of them,' Polly said softly.

'Except mine.' Lydia bit her lip. 'They look at me, and they see guilt. And now I know why.' She sighed heavily. 'I don't know how I'm going to face…'

she couldn't bring herself to say the old name '…Edward. I can't believe they kept something like this from me for all these years.'

'It's not exactly an easy thing to say. And I'm just as guilty. I kept it from you, too,' Polly pointed out.

'At least you tried to get them to tell me. Is that why you had that big row with Mum, when I was sixteen?'

Polly nodded. 'But I realised she wasn't going to give in, and I didn't want to stop seeing you. So I had to compromise.'

'I'm glad you did.' Lydia sighed heavily. 'I have no idea where things are going to go from here. Right now, I don't even want to see them.'

'Let the dust settle,' Polly said. 'Give it a bit of time before you make any decisions.' She hugged Lydia. 'But whatever you decide to do, I'll support you, love.'

'Thank you.'

'I probably shouldn't ask, but has Jake been in touch?'

'No. He didn't even come to my leaving do.' And that really rankled.

'Maybe he was away on business. Did you ask?'

'No.'

'Don't make your mother's mistakes,' Polly said again. 'Pride isn't a virtue. So what if you're the one to ring him? Talk to him. Sort it out.' Polly put a bowl of spaghetti in front of her. 'Things will look better in the morning, love. And you'll come out of this stronger.'

Lydia wasn't so sure, but dutifully dug her fork into her pasta and forced herself to smile.

CHAPTER THIRTEEN

'WHO is it?' Lydia's voice over the intercom sounded tired and harassed.

'Jake.' It was bad timing, from the sound of it. But he'd already left it too long. And right now he really, really needed to see her. 'I need to talk to you. Please. Just give me ten minutes—and then, if you want me to leave, I'll go.'

Her pause lasted so long, he thought she was going to refuse flat out. Then she sighed. 'OK.' She buzzed him up, and was waiting in the doorway when he walked into the landing.

Last time he'd seen her, in the office, she'd been in professional lawyer mode.

Right now, she was wearing faded jeans; her hair was tied back with a scrunchie, with tendrils escaping everywhere, and there was a smudge of pastel on her face. She looked more beautiful than he'd ever seen her, and he wanted to wrap his arms round her and breathe in her scent.

Except he was travel-stained and her face was wary. Now wasn't a good time.

'Temporary apology,' he said, handing her a bunch of roses that were starting to look a bit sorry for themselves. 'They were the best I could get at the airport. I had something else in mind, but I haven't had time to pick it up—and I really needed to see you, Lydia.'

'Come in. And, um, thank you for the flowers.'

He followed her into the kitchen and leaned against the worktop while she put the flowers in water. So, where did he start with the apologies? 'Sorry I didn't come to your leaving do.'

'That's OK.'

He could see from her face that it wasn't. 'I had to go to Norway,' he said. 'My grandfather had a heart attack.'

'Oh, no. Is he all right?'

'It gave the family a scare, but he's on the mend now. And that picture you did for him and my grandmother helped. They asked me to say thank you and to send you their love.' He blew out a breath. 'It's been one hell of a week. And it wasn't what I'd planned, at all. I'd intended to see you on Friday and find out why you refused to have dinner with me.'

She frowned. 'You didn't ask me to have dinner with you.'

'I did. By text, which I know wasn't the best way, but it was two in the morning and I didn't think you'd appreciate a phone call.'

'I didn't get any texts from you.'

He closed his eyes briefly. 'I thought you were just too angry with me to reply.' He sighed. 'Well, the gist of it was that I apologised, told you that you were right and I was wrong, and asked you to have dinner with me. Though I guess it's just as well you didn't get it, because I would've had to cancel at the last minute.'

She blinked, and stared at him. 'I'm in a parallel universe, aren't I?'

'No. I always admit when I'm wrong,' Jake said. 'I'm just not wrong very often.' He grimaced. 'Though I was spectacularly wrong, this time. And last week really brought it home to me—seeing how upset my grandmother was when my grandfather was in hospital, but realising that in the scheme of things that pain was nothing compared to how happy he'd made her in their lives together. And playing with the kids.'

'Kids?'

'My cousins' children,' he explained. 'Someone had to keep them amused while their parents were visiting *Farfar*—the heart ward was a bit strict about not letting kids in.'

She gave him a look of sheer disbelief. 'And *you* entertained them?'

He nodded. 'I had no choice: I had to face up to being around kids for the first time in eighteen months.' He smiled wryly. 'I'd already realised it by then, but it hammered the point home. I know I've made a mess of this, and my timing isn't great—but that picture gave me hope. You see through my skin, Lydia, to the man I could be.' He moistened his lower lip. 'It's a picture of a man in love. And I think—I hope—that the only person who could see through all my barriers and realise that might love me back.' He really, really hoped he hadn't got this wrong. Or it would be utterly disastrous. But it was a risk he needed to take. 'I want you, Lydia. I want you, and I want a family, and I want to live to see my grandchildren grow up.'

'You want *me*?' She looked as if she couldn't quite believe him.

Given the way he'd rejected her in Norway, he could understand why. 'I want you,' he repeated softly. 'Desperately. And for always. You were absolutely right when you told me that I was being impossible and stubborn. I was trying to be noble—and all I was doing was taking your choices away. That wasn't fair, and I'm sorry. I was wrong. And I know it's a lot to ask, but will you give me the chance to make it up to you?'

In answer, she closed the gap between them and wrapped her arms round him.

He buried his face in her hair. 'You smell wonderful. Gardenias.' He sniffed. 'And linseed oil.'

'I forgot!' She looked horrified. 'I'm covered in pastels. Your clothes will be ruined.'

'I don't care. I just need you to hold me.' He rested his cheek against her shoulder. 'I've missed you. This last fortnight's been hell.'

'Tell me about it,' she said dryly. 'Did you make sure you were out of the office on purpose?'

'The first few days, yes,' he admitted. 'I thought it would be easier, not seeing you. But being away from you was torture. I knew what a mistake I'd made—but just when I was going to try and sort it out, Mum rang to say that *Farfar* was in hospital. What could I do?'

'The right thing. Which you did. Your grandparents needed you, and I could wait.' She paused. 'Though you could have phoned me.'

'No. This is something I needed to say face to face. So you could see my eyes.' He pulled back slightly. 'I love you, Lydia. *Jeg elsker deg.* And that's something I'd only say to someone who holds my entire heart.'

I love you.

The words she'd never thought to hear from him.

The words she'd wanted to say…but pride had held her back.

'That doesn't fix everything, I know,' he said. 'There's still a lot we need to talk about. But it's a solid base for working things out. Coming to a compromise that suits us both.'

He'd said it first. And it gave her the courage to answer him. 'I love you, too.'

'Really?'

She stroked his face. 'The more I got to know you, in Norway, the more I fell for you.' She smiled wryly. 'Even though you're difficult and you think you know best.'

'Most of the time,' Jake said, 'I do know best, because I look at the facts and I make logical decisions.'

'You can't live your life by logic—or by cutting people off.'

'I don't cut people off. I'm close to my family.'

She raised an eyebrow. 'Provided they don't talk about a huge list of subjects, that is. Jake, haven't you worked out yet that when people love you, they're prepared to take the rough with the smooth?'

'I'm sorry I hurt you,' He stole a kiss. 'I was trying to give you the chance to find someone who could make you happy. Someone who had a better chance of growing old with you than I do. Except it turns out I'm selfish, and I want to spend the rest of my life with you, however long it lasts.' He dragged in a breath. 'I can't offer you an easy life, Lydia. I don't know how long I'm going to stay in remission, and if the cancer comes back I have no idea whether they'll be able to treat it. My future doesn't come with any certainties.'

'Nobody's does. You can't guarantee that you're not going to be in an accident tomorrow—and neither can I,' she pointed out.

'But it's still a hell of a lot to take on. Grace couldn't handle it.'

She frowned. 'I thought you were the one who broke off your engagement?'

'I was.'

'What aren't you telling me?' she asked, tightening her fingers round his.

'Grace wanted to end it—but she didn't know how. She thought people would blame her for walking out on me.' He shrugged. 'So it was easier on both of us for me to do it. And I can't blame her. She wanted kids and I couldn't give them to her.'

Lydia stared at him in disbelief. 'Jake, you'd just been diagnosed with cancer and you needed her support. She was your fiancée, for pity's sake—the woman who'd planned to spend the rest of her life with you. How could she let you down at a time like that?'

'Because she was scared, Lydia. For all she knew, if she married me, she could have been a widow a couple of years down the line. It's a lot to ask.'

'If you love someone, you stand by…' Her voice faded. Who was she to argue? Robbie hadn't loved her enough to stand by her or stand up to her parents. Yes, her father had stood by her mother— but did Edward actually love Ruth? She had no idea.

'That's the point, *min kjære*. Grace didn't love me enough. I wouldn't have made her happy, and she would have made me miserable. Sure, I was bitter about it at first, but I had plenty of time to think about it and come to terms with it.' He looked away. 'She's married, now. With a nine-month-old baby.'

Lydia winced. 'That must have hurt when you found out.'

'It did. For a while. But she wasn't the one for me. And now I know she did me a favour, because I've found the person I really do want to spend my life with.' He turned to look her straight in the eye. 'As I said, I owe you an apology—for not giving you the chance to show me that you weren't Grace.'

He'd filled in some gaps. It was time she did, too. 'And I didn't give you the chance to show me that you weren't Robbie,' she said quietly.

'Robbie?' he asked gently.

She told him the whole sordid story. Quietly and succinctly.

Jake looked at her, disbelief written all over his face. 'He actually *took* the cheque from your father?'

She nodded.

'What a…' He said something in Norwegian that she guessed was highly uncomplimentary.

'He was young, Jake. He made mistakes.' Just as her biological father had.

'He hurt you. And as for your father—'

'He did me a favour, in the long run,' she cut in gently. 'Robbie wasn't the right one for me, and I would've been miserable with him. He would've let me down.'

'But your father took your choices away. So did Robbie. Why didn't you tell me before?'

'Because I was ashamed,' she admitted.

'Why? You had nothing to be ashamed about. They both let you down.' He paused. 'Hang on. You thought that you weren't good enough for Robbie, didn't you? That he picked the money over you, because you weren't worth it.'

She flushed. 'Do we have to talk about this?'

'Yes, we do. Listen to me, Lydia. You're enough, all right. Robbie was the one with the poor judgement. He didn't see you for who you are, and your parents don't either.' He curled his fingers round hers. 'You did the right thing, changing your career. You were a perfectly competent lawyer—but you're a much better artist, because your passion for your work shines through.' His gaze held hers. 'I believe in you.'

His face, his voice, were utterly sincere.

He believed in her.

And it felt as if something had just cracked inside her. 'Jake,' she whispered. 'I believe in you, too. OK, so we might not have years and years, like your grandparents have. But I'm willing to take that risk. I want every second of the time we have left together.'

He drew her close, and she realised that he was shuddering.

'Do you know what you're offering to give up, Lydia?' His voice was hoarse. 'I know you want children. You told me. And I…I can't give you that. Well, not without a lot of help.'

'Help?'

'The doctors froze some of my sperm before I had the radiotherapy—at the time I didn't think there was any point, but they said I was young and they wanted me to keep my options open.'

'So we could try IVF,' she said thoughtfully.

He shook his head. 'There aren't any guarantees. I've read up about it since the operation. There's only a one in four chance that it'll work—and it means you'll have to take all kinds of hormones, a series of painful injections, and then have a general anaesthetic when they harvest the eggs and…' He dragged in a breath. 'I don't want to put you through that. The physical and emotional stresses are just too much.'

'I thought you promised to stop being noble?'

'It's the sensible decision.'

'But it's not the only option.'

He frowned. 'Grace couldn't face it.'

'I'm not Grace. And you're not Robbie.'

He blinked. 'Are you telling me you'd put yourself through all that?'

'I'd consider it, Jake. Because I'd love to have a child who looks just like you. But there are other ways,' she said softly. 'Being a parent isn't just about giving birth. If we do decide to try IVF—and we're going to have to talk about it a lot more first, and make that decision *together*—and it doesn't work, we can still foster or adopt. It doesn't mean we'll love our children less if they're not biologically ours. They'll still be our child, in our hearts.'

'That's true.' He stroked her face. 'But I can still see doubts in your eyes.'

'I don't know if I'm going to be any good as a mother,' she admitted.

He smiled. 'I've seen you with children. So I can tell you now, you'll be great. Why on earth do you think you wouldn't?'

She stared at the floor. 'You grew up knowing your parents loved you. I didn't.'

He kissed the tip of her nose. 'Of course they loved you. Maybe they weren't any good at showing it. But you'll be good at showing it.' He drew her closer. 'Because you're not your parents. You're you.'

'No, Jake.' She bit her lip. 'I always knew I wasn't planned, and I thought my parents were disappointed because I wasn't a boy. That's one of the reasons I became a lawyer—to show them that I could follow in their footsteps, that I could make them just as proud as a boy could've done.'

'You're a woman to be proud of, *elskling*. You don't disappoint me, you won't disappoint my family, and you won't disappoint our children, if we're blessed.'

'That's not what I'm trying to tell you.' She dragged in a breath. 'I found out the truth, yesterday. I'm not my father's child.' She told him what she'd learned from Ruth.

'Oh, honey.' Jake held her close. 'That must have been a hell of a shock.'

'I'm still coming to terms with it,' she said. 'But I think I understand them both more. For my father, I was living proof of how his marriage had almost failed, and how he'd always been second best in my mother's eyes. And it must've been twisting the knife when I turned out to be good at art. My mother felt guilty for betraying him, so she backed him.'

'And you were left caught in the middle, not knowing what was going on and thinking that you didn't measure up as a daughter.' Jake stroked her face. 'Whereas, actually, you more than measure up.'

'They didn't love me, Jake, because they didn't know how. There wasn't room between the guilt and the resentment.'

'That's the thing about love,' Jake said. 'It *makes* room. And there's definitely room in my family for you. My grandparents already adore you. My parents will love you. And I…' He stopped. 'Part of me wants to whisk you back to Norway, find the Northern Lights, and then make a huge declaration under them. But it's all just window dressing. So I'm going to cut to the important stuff. I love you, Lydia Sheridan. With all my heart. I want to be a family with you. I know I'm not offering you an easy future, but will you marry me?'

He'd said he loved her with all his heart.

And he was giving her the choice. The option to say no. Or…

'Yes,' she said.

And then he was holding her so tightly, kissing her deeply. But she was holding on to him just as tightly, so it was fine.

He was shaking when he finally broke the kiss. 'You'll really take that chance on me?'

'The alternative—being without you—is unbearable,' she said simply. 'Sure, we'll have rough times ahead. But we'll have good times, too. They'll help to see us through the bad stuff.'

'And from now on,' Jake said, 'I'll do everything in my power to make your dreams come true. I can't promise you the moon and stars—but I'll be there beside you all the way.'

Three days later, Jake was by Lydia's side as they walked into St Pancras Cemetery. From the information that Polly had supplied, they'd been able to find exactly where Daniel was buried.

The grave had been tended; Lydia had no idea whether Daniel's family had done it, or whether her mother had.

Not that it mattered. The main thing was that he hadn't been forgotten.

She lay the bunch of white lilies in front of the gravestone and took a step back. 'I'm sorry I haven't been before. I didn't know about you,' she said. 'But I do now. So I'll come back again, if that's OK.'

Crazy. Talking to a grave of a man she'd never met. Her father.

But Jake was beside her, holding her hand. He understood. And Lydia drew strength from that.

'I'm sorry we didn't get to meet. Polly says we would've liked each other. And I hope,' she said, 'that you would've been proud of me.'

Jake's fingers tightened round hers, as if to tell her that of course he would.

She stared at the headstone. 'I'll come back again,' she said softly.

Jake didn't push her to talk as they walked back out of the cemetery, but he did steer her across the road to a café.

'Thanks for coming with me,' she said as he set her coffee in front of her. 'Especially as I know you're really busy, right now.'

'You don't think I would've let you go alone, the first time, do you?' he asked. 'And anyway, it's about time I gave my deputy a bit more responsibility instead of being such a control freak.'

'You said it.' But he'd made her smile. She looked at him, and frowned. 'What's wrong?'

'Nothing.'

'Jake. You promised. No more being noble. Don't shut me out.'

He sighed. 'It's morbid.'

'We've just visited a cemetery. You're allowed to be morbid.'

He reached across the table and held her hand. 'OK. Since you asked, the way you just talked to your father… One day, you might be talking like that to me. And if we have children, one day they'll…' He broke off.

Her fingers tightened round his. 'I'd rather have you and love you for as long as we get, than not have you at all. And of course I'll come and talk to you— just as I hope you'll come and talk to me if I go first.'

'Sorry. Every so often, the fear comes back.'

'I know,' she said softly. 'I hope we'll get our lifetime together. But if we don't, I'll treasure the time we do have. And I'll be able to tell our children the things I don't know about my own father. I'll have answers for their questions. I can tell them you're the love of my life, and you were proud of them.' She blinked away the threatening tears. 'And we'll have photos and film and lots and lots of memories. They'll be able to see you and hear you just as you are now.'

'Yeah.' He fumbled in the pocket of his coat and drew out a box; he pushed it across the table to her. 'Talking about memories… I picked this up, this morning. For you.'

The box was too big to contain an engagement ring; besides, they'd agreed to choose one together.

She opened it, and was amazed to see a silver and

glass bracelet inside the box. 'Jake, it's beautiful. I saw one like this in Oslo.'

'I remembered. Though you wouldn't be able to get one *quite* like this. Most of the beads are one-offs.'

She felt her eyes widen. 'You commissioned it?'

He nodded. 'The designs are all things from the first week we spent together.'

She looked at the beads more closely. 'The ship museum,' she said, recognising the design from the prow of the ship on one bead, and what looked like a midnight sun marked in gold, with rays radiating out. 'Is that iolite in the centre?'

'Yes.'

She continued looking. A turquoise bead like the light in their room in the ice hotel. A swirly glass bead with the colours that radiated from the Munch 'Madonna'—the same colours she'd used to paint him. A delicate snowflake. A glass bead that reminded her of the fir trees against the snow from their dog-sledding trip. An abstract like the roof of the Arctic Cathedral.

'All those memories,' she said softly. He'd put so much thought into it. Made it personal—for them.

'That's what Scandinavian charm bracelets are for. Memories. Though it's deliberately not full, because we still have some memories to make together.' He leaned across the table and stole a kiss. 'I have a glass bead for a memory we're going to make very soon. It's black and green.'

'For the Northern Lights,' she guessed.

'I promised to take you to see them, and I will. And I'd like to give you a bead to match your wedding ring, on our wedding day.'

'Jake, that's...' Her eyes filled with tears. 'Nobody's ever put that much thought into something for me before.'

'*Jeg elsker deg,*' he said. 'I did it because I love you.'

'I love you too, Jake.'

'May I?' he asked, indicating the bracelet.

She nodded, and he bared her wrist; he pressed his mouth to her pulse point briefly before clipping the bracelet on. 'Memories,' he said softly. 'And may these be the first of many happy ones for you and me.'

CHAPTER FOURTEEN

'What, now?'

'Now,' Jake confirmed.

'But—we can't just leave, Jake. We haven't had the first dance yet!'

'It's our wedding reception, Mrs Andersen.' Jake laughed. 'So I think that means we can do whatever we like.'

And what a wedding it had been.

Quite how Jake had managed to organise the wedding of her dreams in all of two months, Lydia had no idea. But he'd done it. Polly had designed her wedding dress and Emma's deep blue maid of honour dress; Astrid had sorted out the flowers, and Jake had sorted out everything else over the phone. Jake hadn't wanted to wait to get married and, as Per wasn't allowed to fly for a couple more months, it had made sense for them to get married in Norway.

But the one thing that had worried Lydia was the fact that the church would be practically empty, on her side. She'd have only Polly, Natasha, Emma's husband Mike, a couple of friends and Emma, when she wasn't doing matron-of-honour duties.

As for her parents… She'd sent them an invitation to the wedding, but there had been no reply. Not that she'd really expected one.

'It doesn't matter,' Jake said firmly when she finally confessed her worries to him. 'My family is your family—and they're not waiting until the wedding to claim you as theirs, either.' Jake's parents had been just as warm and welcoming as Astrid and Per, immediately taking her to their hearts.

So she'd flown to Norway with Polly, Emma, Natasha and Mike. Stayed in the hotel where they were holding the reception. Allowed Polly, Emma and Natasha to dress her up and paint her nails and take endless photographs.

Jake had sent her a deep red rose, that morning. Attached to it was an envelope containing a silver bead in the shape of a rose, and a note. *'To make you think of getting dressed on our wedding morning. I love you.'*

And when Emma came to tell her that the car was waiting, she handed Lydia another envelope.

'To remember your journey to the church,' was the message wrapped around another bead.

Lydia inspected the bead, mystified. A reindeer?

And then Emma led her outside. Waiting for her was a sleigh, pulled by four reindeer.

'He's definitely Prince Charming,' Emma said.

'Believe me, this is the most fairy-tale wedding I could ever imagine.'

And her husband-to-be was full of surprises. Because when she arrived at the church, someone she really hadn't expected to see stepped out of the porch.

'You look beautiful, just as I always thought my daughter would look on her wedding day,' Edward Sheridan told her.

The lump in Lydia's throat was so huge that she couldn't say a word.

'I owe you an apology.' Edward said. 'This isn't the time or place to have that conversation, but we'll talk some time soon. But I do want you to know that your mother and I are so sorry that we've hurt you. And, if you'll let me, I'd be proud to walk down the aisle beside you to Jake.'

Lydia blinked back her tears and nodded.

'This is the proudest moment of my life, better even than when I made QC,' Edward said, taking her arm. 'Because I know you're marrying a man who loves you the way you should be loved.'

How had Jake managed this? To give her the father she'd always wanted, but who'd always made her feel that she never measured up? 'What—what did Jake say to you?' Lydia asked, her voice cracked.

'That's between him and me. But let's just say that I'd hate to be against him in a court of law,' Edward said dryly. 'He's very…perceptive.'

'He's a lot of things.'

'As long as you're sure about this and he makes you happy.'

'He does.'

'Then let's get this wedding under way,' Edward said softly. 'I hope Polly has extra tissues. Your mother might need them.'

And as the church doors opened and the congregation stood Lydia walked down the aisle to Jake—who was waiting for her by the altar, his eyes filled with love. A love that Lydia felt shone all the way through her, too; now she understood why brides were always described as 'radiant'.

And her voice had been very clear in her vows. 'In sickness and in health…'

The reception, too, had been a dream. Wonderful food, and a cake that Astrid had made herself: a traditional Norwegian wedding cake, the *kranskake*, made from a tower of rings, with icing trickling down like a waterfall and studded with edible flowers. Speeches that made everyone laugh. Jake doing a double act with his grandfather and making the children shriek with laughter. Jake's mother hugging her: 'You've given us our son back, as well as becoming the daughter I've always wanted.' Memories that Lydia would have and hold for ever.

And now Jake was proposing that they should sneak out and leave everyone to the dancing?

'We'll be back in time for the first dance,' Jake

said. 'I built a two-hour gap between the formal meal and the evening reception. People are going to take the chance of having a nap in their room—or, knowing my family, they'll sit round drinking coffee and reminiscing about every family wedding for the last fifty years. The kids are going to have a magic show to keep them amused, and nobody will notice if we disappear for a little while.' He smiled. 'I want to show you something.'

'You've already given me the best day of my life,' Lydia said. 'So I'll trust your judgement.'

'Good.' He led her to their room. 'Let me help you out of that dress, Mrs Andersen.'

Lydia burst out laughing. 'Jakob, are you telling me that we're going to consummate our wedding right now?'

'I'm planning *that* for later,' he told her, laughing back. 'No. This is window dressing. *Important* window dressing.' He gestured to the pile of clothes on the bed.

'Thermals?'

'Trust me,' he said. 'You'll need them.'

She allowed him to help her out of the dress and into the warm clothing, and waited while he stripped.

'What?' he asked.

'Just thinking what a lovely picture that would make. Natasha said my life studies are going very well, but she thinks I need practice. So I need to find some life models.'

'Model,' Jake corrected. 'The only naked man you draw is me.'

'Why, thank you, honey. I accept your offer to pose for me,' she teased.

'Very funny.' Jake shepherded her out to the car he'd hired earlier.

Guessing exactly what Jake meant by 'window dressing', Lydia glanced up at the sky. 'It's completely overcast.' He couldn't possibly think they had a chance of seeing the Northern Lights in the next two hours. 'Jake, it's a lovely thought, but it's not going to happen. We spent a whole week here in December, and didn't see so much as a single flicker.'

'February's the best month. And let's just say I have a feeling.'

'A feeling?'

He smiled. 'All right. I've been obsessively checking the weather forecast, so I'm about as sure as I can be.' He drove them away from the town, and stopped by the fjord. 'Right. We need the snowsuits.'

They helped each other into the final layer. And when they stepped outside the car, Lydia saw there was a break in the clouds. The stars were brighter than she'd ever seen them, and as the clouds slowly dispersed the stars were reflected in the fjord. Dazzling.

'This is beautiful, Jake.'

'Not as beautiful as my bride. Happy wedding

day, *min kjære*.' He wrapped his arms round her waist, drawing her back against his body. 'Look up,' he directed softly.

She did so, and she was awed into speechlessness. Above them, there was a faint streak of green.

A streak that slowly became wider and brighter and began to curl above them, rippling down into a curtain that stretched across the horizon. The stars glittered through the eerie green glow, and as she looked out over the fjord Lydia could see the reflections of the Northern Lights dancing. She watched, amazed, as the lights flickered above them; spreading out like a wide and soft mist, then narrowing down into an intensely bright streak, swirling through the blackness of the sky. Every now and then, there was a faint wash of red. And she'd never seen anything so amazing in her entire life. A light show that glowed through the whole of the heavens.

'I know you always wanted to see the Northern Lights, and I promised you I'd make all your dreams come true, as much as it's in my power to do it,' Jake said softly. 'And today, our wedding day, I really wanted this to happen.'

'Jake, you've given me so much. Every single dream.'

'And you've given me my dreams back. I love you, Lyddie. With all my heart.'

'Oh, Jake.' He'd called her 'Lyddie'. Not

elskling or *min kjære*—beautiful endearments, but ones that could be used for anyone. This was personal. Like her bracelet. Her eyes filled with tears, blurring the incredible spectacle above her. 'I love you, too. So much.'

When the lights faded, Lydia was still close to tears.

'Let's go and thaw out,' he said softly, keeping his arms round her as he shepherded her back to the car.

'That was…' She shook her head, barely able to explain how she felt. He'd shown her the one thing she'd always dreamed about seeing—and on such a special day. 'I'm…I'm overwhelmed.'

'I know, *min kjære*,' he said. 'Me, too.' He helped her out of her snowsuit, then wriggled out of his, and drove them back to the hotel.

It took a long, long time for him to help her out of her clothes. And even longer before he helped her back into her wedding dress. 'Jakob Andersen, you're beyond my wildest dreams,' she said softly, stealing a final kiss.

'Just as you're beyond mine.' He unpinned her hair. 'You looked beautiful with it up, but I like your hair down. And very slightly ruffled.' He kissed her lingeringly. 'My beautiful wife. I love you just the way you are. But, much as I'd like you all to myself, we'd better go back to our guests. They won't start the dancing without us.'

As they walked back into the reception room the toastmaster rang a bell, silencing everyone.

'Ladies and gentlemen,' he said, 'I give you the bride and groom. Mr and Mrs Jake Andersen.'

And the room erupted in champagne and confetti.

EPILOGUE

Eighteen months later

JAKE gently laid the month-old baby on the mattress and tucked him in. 'Tell me again, Mrs Andersen, how did we manage to make such a beautiful son?'

'Because his father has the sexiest mouth in the universe, and eyes the colour of an Arctic summer sky,' Lydia said promptly.

'So it's nothing to do with the fact that his mother is the most beautiful woman in the world? Not to mention the most talented, clever, award-winning artist?'

'Jake, it wasn't a huge award.' She flapped a dismissive hand. 'It wasn't in the league of the Turner Prize or an exhibition at the Tate Modern.'

'It still counts. And I'm terribly proud of you. Tell her, Edward Jakob Daniel Andersen,' he addressed his son. 'Tell your mother that she's a superstar and we think she's brilliant.'

The baby gurgled.

'That was babytalk for "Dad, you're absolutely right,"' Jake told her with a smile. He leaned on the edge of the cot. 'Our beautiful boy. Our miracle child. You've given me everything, Lyddie. Love and faith and the family I always wanted. And you were so brave during the IVF.'

Lydia moved to stand beside him, looping her arm round his waist at the same moment that he curved one arm round her shoulders. 'Hey. I wouldn't have done it if I hadn't wanted it as much as you did. And you held my hand all the way.'

And he'd held her close, the day they'd found out that the first cycle of treatment hadn't worked. Held her while she'd cried, been strong for her. And let his own tears mingle with hers; she'd made him strong enough not to fear showing his feelings any more.

'But we've had good times as well as bad,' he said. One of the best being the day before, at his hospital review, where his consultant had told him to come back in two years' time. His remission was holding.

'We certainly have.' She drew him closer. 'And maybe we can adopt a little brother or sister for Ed, in the future—he's already practically got a big brother and sister with Lawrence's two.' She smiled. 'You've shown me that love makes room. We'll love our other children just as much as we love him. It won't be like my parents were with me—no guilt, no blame.'

'Your dad was so pleased to think we called the

baby after him. You're not going to tell him the truth, are you?'

'That I went for the English version of a certain artist's first name, because painting you in his style was the moment I realised I'd fallen for you? No,' Lydia said. 'My parents made a lot of mistakes with me, but I need to give them the chance to get it right this time round. With their grandchildren.' And they'd made an effort with her. Apologised for the way they'd made her feel over the years. Jake still refused to tell her exactly what he'd said to her parents, but from her wedding day onwards Edward and Ruth had finally seemed to value Lydia for who she was.

'They seem happier together, too,' Jake said. 'More relaxed with each other.'

'I think it was seeing what your parents and your grandparents have, and realising that they could have it too, if they stopped punishing each other,' she said reflectively. 'It's a shame they couldn't have seen it years ago.'

'Glass half full,' he said. 'If they had, you wouldn't have worked at Andersen's—and we might never have met.'

She shivered. 'Now that's a seriously scary thought. You're going to have to make it up to me, for terrifying me.'

'Uh-oh. I think your mother's planning to have her wicked way with me in her studio,' Jake told the baby. 'So it's just as well you need a nap.'

As if on cue, Edward yawned widely.

'Sleep well, little one,' Lydia said, stroking his soft cheek with the backs of her fingers. 'And remember your mum and dad love you more than words can say.'

She leaned over to wind up the lullaby light show. As the first notes of Brahms's 'Lullaby' floated into the air Jake closed the curtains. Lydia switched on the baby listener, and together they tiptoed out of the nursery and into the studio at the back of the house.

Jake drew the blinds as Lydia untucked his shirt and splayed her palms across his bare skin.

'Mmm. Gorgeous, and all mine,' she said with a grin.

'Just as you're gorgeous, and all mine,' he said, twisting round so he could kiss her deeply. 'Always.'

* * * * *

*Harlequin Presents® is thrilled to introduce
sparkling new talent Caitlin Crews!
Caitlin's debut book is a fast-paced, intense story,
with a gorgeous Italian hero, a defiant princess
and plenty of passion and seduction!*

*Available next month in Harlequin Presents:
PURE PRINCESS, BARTERED BRIDE*

"YOU HAVE MADE him proud," he told her, nodding at her father, feeling benevolent. "You are the jewel of his kingdom."

Finally, she turned her head and met his gaze, her sea-colored eyes were clear and grave as she regarded him.

"Some jewels are prized for their sentimental value," she said, her musical voice pitched low, but not low enough to hide the faint tremor in it. "And others for their monetary value."

"You are invaluable," he told her, assuming that would be the end of it. Didn't women love such compliments? He'd never bothered to give them before. But Gabrielle shrugged, her mouth tightening.

"Who is to say what my father values?" she asked, her light tone unconvincing. "I would be the last to know."

"But I know," he said.

"Yes." Again, that grave, sea-green gaze. "I am invaluable, a jewel without price." She looked away. "And yet, somehow, contracts were drawn up, a price agreed upon and here we are."

There was the taint of bitterness to her words then. Luc frowned. He should not have indulged her—he regretted the impulse. This was what happened when emotions were given reign.

"Tell me, princess," he said, leaning close, enjoying the way her eyes widened, though she did not back away from him. He liked her show of courage, but he wanted to make his point perfectly clear. "What was your expectation? Do not speak to me of contracts and prices in this way, as if you are the victim of some subterfuge," he ordered her, harshly. "You insult us both."

Her gaze flew to his, and he read the crackling temper there. It intrigued him as much as it annoyed him—but either way he could not allow it. There could be no rebellion, no bitterness, no intrigue in this marriage. There could only be his will and her surrender.

He remembered where they were only because the band chose that moment to begin playing. He sat back in his chair, away from her. *She is not merely a business acquisition,* he told himself, once more grappling with the urge to protect her—safeguard her. *She is not a hotel, or a company.*

She was his wife. He could allow her more leeway than he would allow the other things he controlled. At least today.

"No more of this," he said, rising to his feet. She looked at him warily. He extended his hand to her and smiled. He could be charming if he chose. "I believe it is time for me to dance with my wife."

Indulge yourself with this passionate love story that starts out as a royal marriage of convenience, and look out for more dramatic books from Caitlin Crews and Harlequin Presents in 2010!